F. Vernon White

First and Last

A novel

F. Vernon White

First and Last
A novel

ISBN/EAN: 9783337042929

Printed in Europe, USA, Canada, Australia, Japan

Cover: Foto ©Andreas Hilbeck / pixelio.de

More available books at **www.hansebooks.com**

FIRST AND LAST.

FIRST AND LAST.

A Novel.

By F. VERNON WHITE.

IN TWO VOLUMES.

VOL II.

LONDON:

SAMUEL TINSLEY, SOUTHAMPTON ST., STRAND.

1873.

MANCHESTER:
JOHN HEYWOOD, EXCELSIOR PRINTING WORKS,
HULME HALL ROAD.

CONTENTS.

FIRST AND LAST.

CHAPTER I.

'A PARABLE.'

THE one virtue which I think the upper classes may almost arrogate to themselves is their faculty of taking their own or their friends' misfortunes coolly; that is, I mean to say, with apparent calmness. I daresay they really *feel* as much as their less aristocratic brethren. If a vulgar person is in love, he can't help showing it in the most idiotic manner to every acquaintance; if a *parvenu* has lost his fortune, he betrays it on every feature; but people of *ton* lose their hearts, and their money too, without the movement of a muscle.

It is a great blessing this control over our emotions, for it enables us to hoodwink our neighbours so successfully. I think no man could have been more hopelessly in love than Hammersley was with his fair hostess; but he had been so well trained in the world of fashion, that I would have defied the keenest looker-on to have guessed it. The 'grand passion' had cost him some misery up till now, but he was not going to exhibit his weakness to the world.

Without any effort of his own, he confirmed and increased the good opinion which his host had formed of him in the morning, so much so, that Ardross afterwards declared in private to his wife that he was one of the best fellows he had ever known. I think there is sometimes a certain infatuation prevalent amongst these big, good-natured, guileless men, that makes them apt to take a fancy to their worst enemies. Ardross evidently did not share in those suspicions which most worldly people entertain with regard to those convenient relations yclept cousins.

But, then, some allowance must be made for him. He had never been, like the majority of his contemporaries, to a public school, and any of my readers whose brothers or husbands have graduated in these nurseries of worldly youth will readily understand the defects in his education. If you want a boy to be versed in the science of suspicion, which a daily mixing among our fellow-creatures, unfortunately, too often compels, by all means send him to a public school, and it is long odds that he will enter the adult world with an experience to which little can be added. He had mixed sufficiently among London men after his majority to become tolerably acquainted with the world, but his opinion of it had not been rendered very favourable thereby. He had found the majority of women contesting a keen race for supremacy in the things that seemed to constitute their ambition—the worship of the idols of wood and stone that society sets up for its gods—and ready to whisper all manner of evil concerning their rivals; and he had found the tongues of his own sex more foul, if less bitter, than those of the other. The fair fame of one of their own order was as little sacred from the scandal of the clubs as the slightness of the materials on which they based their scandal was an impediment to its full circulation as an undoubted fact.

He had heard, therefore, so much vice hinted at in others that he had almost grown to disbelieve in its existence, for it seemed to him that if all the men and women were one-half as bad as their acquaintances painted them, it would be impossible that the world could contain such iniquity a moment longer. I do not say that, in a worldly sense, he might not have erred as much on the side of leniency as others on the side of severity ; but, if I must choose between the two, I would sooner have an enthusiast than a sceptic. There is *something* noble about a man who still believes in the capacity of his fellow-creatures for good, while the cold-blooded cynic, who is for ever making out mankind as worse in their impulses and passions than the devils, is a hideous travestie of the creation he despises.

So Hammersley soon became the *ami de la*

maison, dining often with Ardross, and
dropping in of afternoons, at first with decent
intervals between the visits, and then a great
deal more often than would have been safe
with a less unsuspicious husband. I am not
one of those sceptics who disbelieve in friendship between a man and a woman ; on the
contrary, I think there are many who enjoy a
connection of this kind without an *arrière
pensée* of evil ; but friendship, like everything
else, has its limits ; and were I a husband, and
found any male acquaintance giving to my
wife as much time as I gave her when a lover,
I certainly should think it time to investigate
the matter.

Ardross, however, never seemed to look
upon the intimacy between his wife and her
cousin as anything too pronounced for inno-
cence, and Edith made no attempt to diminish
the intervals between his visits, although she
knew now, if she did not before, the full
strength of her love for him—knew it the
more, perhaps, from the fact that she could
contrast it with what she felt for her husband.
She knew well that the most passionate

caress of her lawful lover could never waken
in her one-tenth of the emotion that the most
careless glance of the other could arouse. She
felt for the one esteem and love, such as a
child may feel for its parent, as a sister may
feel for a favourite brother; but the other
she loved with a deep, passionate, and abiding
love, that had something almost terrible in its
intensity.

And still she had not shown it him as yet.
Though he sat opposite to her day after day—
day after day took her hand and looked in her
eyes—he could not divine the depth of her
passion; and she tried to comfort herself with
this, though her conscience pricked her sorely :
for Edith, as I have said, was not a wicked
woman at heart, and these visits seemed a
foul treason to her husband's trust in her ; but
she was weaker now than she had been in
the old days. The sin was so attractive she
could not fly from it ; and she tried to persuade
herself that if she were loyal in deed and word
to her husband, her weakness would be forgiven her. How many wives have reasoned
thus, and stood less staunchly by their notions

of honour, false though they were, than Edith?

And Hammersley was to the full as passionately enamoured of her as in the old days,
save that a certain longing for revenge
mingled with his love. He felt that, whatever future sacrifices she might make for him,
he could never pardon that one desertion—
he could never forgive her taking another
man as husband—bestowing on another the
caresses that should have been given only
to him. It was to him the same as if she
had been unfaithful as a wife. According
to his stern and fantastic morality, they had
been as much wedded from the fact of their
intense love as if their union had been
solemnised with all the pomp and rites of the
Church.

He had tried hard to get some confession
out of Edith that could indicate the precise
degree of her affection for him, but hitherto
she had baffled all his efforts, frequent and
often skilful as they were. She knew, if a
woman once says ' I love you,' what a hold it
gives a man over her; it gives him almost a
double right to plead—for her happiness as well

as his own; and Hammersley was the last who
would have scrupled at using the assistance
her weakness afforded him. If she would
still keep loyal to her husband—and heaven
alone knows the struggle in a woman's heart
where duty whispers 'I must,' and passion is
almost constrained to reply 'I cannot'—she
must rely alone on her own strength. She
had a double task to perform—to conquer her
own love as best she might, and contend
against his.

She had done this hitherto pretty well:
subtle sometimes as the questions were to
which he hoped to get the one answer, she
had always contrived to baffle him. Only the
day before, when he had fancied there was no
escape for her, she had eluded him at the
last moment, leaving him as much in the dark
as ever, and he had left the house with a
bitter sense of failure on him, to think that,
with all his man's superior intellect and
cunning, he should be foiled by a woman's
finesse. 'By G—d, she *shall* speak!' he had
cried passionately to himself: 'I will not be
baffled like this for ever, after all the torture

she has made me suffer. She has trampled on my heart long enough ; it is time I drew the mask from hers.'

And next day he did contrive to lift the mask, not much it is true compared with his success of afterwards, but just enough to give him encouragement in prosecuting the crusade against her honour which he had deliberately set himself to accomplish. They were sitting alone together, the earl being out somewhere— he was generally invisible on afternoons. There had been silence between them for a few moments, which interval Hammersley employed to indulge in a reverie, seemingly so very intense that it attracted his cousin's observation.

'What hath chanced to-day that Cæsar looks so sad ?' she asked, playfully. Had she known the turn that question was going to give to the conversation she would most assuredly have repressed her curiosity.

'I was thinking of old times,' he said, gravely. 'Some people like to remember the "days that are gone," I believe. I find them particularly unpleasant memories, I am sorry to say.'

She knew well enough what that meant, and was at her wits' ends how to answer diplomatically, as usual on such occasions. The remark she made only served to make matters much worse.

'I don't see why you should,' she said, in her embarrassment.

Her cousin drew his chair rather closer to her, and looked her full in the face, very gravely and very sternly.

'You don't seem to understand why I should find the memories of old days unpleasant?' he said, quietly. 'Well, suppose I make it clear to you by a little parable; will you promise to listen?'

She bent her head in acquiescence, with a strange uneasiness as to the result of this deliberate prelude. Was she going to be taken off her guard at last, so long and well as she had kept him at bay?

'It's a fine institution the parable,' he continued, when she had signified her intention to listen. 'It is the way One greater than man

used to get His meaning into the Jews, who
couldn't, or wouldn't—it is much the same
thing in the end—understand Him otherwise;
and perhaps I may succeed in enlightening
you by the same means. Well, then, here is
my parable: A certain man had a favourite
bird that he had bought when he was a boy,
and whom he had fed and tended himself
from the hour he had him. And this bird
was his dearest companion. He would take
his food from no other hand, and he would
nestle in his master's bosom; and if, as it
sometimes chanced—for transient grief will
sometimes cloud the brightest lives—he was
sad, this little bird would pour forth his
sweetest songs, until the shadow vanished
from his master's brow. And thus these two
had grown so dear to each other, that the man
thought none other would take his place.
But one day there came other guests to the
master's house, and they admired his treasure, praised his plumage and his songs, and
stroked him and caressed him; and the bird
seemed to rejoice in their caressings and
praises, insomuch as he did not care to come

to his old friend as much as formerly, till at
last he would not suffer any but the strangers
to pet him ; and the master went away broken-
hearted, because he loved him no longer.
Have you followed me so far ?'

She bowed her head. She had grown very
pale over this recital, for, few and homely as
the words were, the intense feeling with which
he spoke gave them a deep significance. He
noted this, and a feeling of triumph for the
first time came over him. His parable was
evidently taking effect. He went on even
more impressively :

'So the master went far away, hoping that
time and absence would repair the wound that
the treachery of his favourite had caused him ;
but, though he knew how unworthy the bird
was, he could not banish it from his thoughts,
but it haunted him day and night, and at last,
in his wanderings, all undertaken in hopes
that he might find peace, he came to a city
where he met one of the guests who had
petted his favourite, and then he learned that
the bird whom he had loved and cherished so
long was with him. And he went home with

his friend to see him, for he could not go away without one glimpse of the thing that was so very dear ; and he saw him feed from his new master's hand, and nestle in his bosom, and sing his sweetest songs, the same as he had done long ago to him. And when he saw this, and thought of the bygone days when those two were one in heart and love, when they lived only for each other, and contrasted them with the bitter picture of now, what wonder that he looked sad and heartbroken. Can you sympathise with my parable, Edith ? Can you pity the man who found his treasure, that he had loved so dearly, in the hands of another ?'

She had buried her face in her hands, and was sobbing bitterly. He had touched the chord at last ; he had opened alike the floodgates of memory and remorse. She felt as David may have felt when Nathan brought his sin home to him with that parable of the ewe-lamb. She knew that she had dealt moral death to her lover. Never had she felt her treachery as she did then.

He stooped down to take her hands away,

but she held them firmly over her face, sobbing
all the while.

'Edith,' he said, and the voice that had just
now been bitter in its implied accusation
trembled with the intensity of his passion,
'do you recognise the parable at last? Do
you know now why the memories of the past
are so painful? You, you are the treasure
that I doted on, that I hoarded and hugged
to myself as a miser does his gold, fearful that
a human eye shall light upon it and rob him.
And now I find you the darling of another,
petted and caressed by him as you were by
me in the days gone by ; and yet, Edith, God
be my witness, in spite of your treachery and
treason to my heart, I love you still.'

His voice almost broke into a sob as he
ended with that avowal. His fancied sense
of wrong, the half hate mingling with his love,
all vanished in presence of the unutterable
passion with which this woman inspired him.

'Oh, Fred,' she wailed, presently, in her
utter abandonment of sorrow, 'can you forgive
me for the injury I have done you?'

'I will forget and forgive everything you

have done,' he cried eagerly, 'if you will only tell me you love me still.'

She pushed the heavy masses of hair back from her forehead with the quick, convulsive gesture of a person labouring under some awful emotion, and rose from her seat.

'Leave me, for God's sake leave me!' she said; 'I cannot tell you now—another time—but—but—go now.'

She sank back quivering on the chair from which she had just risen. No pride left in her now. Once more he attempted to urge that question.

Her eyes sparkled with a strange, unnatural light, a light that must gleam in the eyes of hunted creatures when they are brought to bay.

'If you have one spark of pity or love left in you,' she cried, passionately, 'don't assist one moment longer in the spectacle of my humiliation. Come to-night—to-morrow—any time when I can be mistress of myself—but do not stay now.'

He passed out of the room, and was soon

in the busy streets of Paris, reviewing the previous scene in his mind.

'She loves me still,' he murmured to himself, with triumph in his tone. 'Whatever her motive for marrying Ardross, I have the best part of her heart. That was genuine emotion to-day: Edith wouldn't sham sentiment for the mere sake of humiliating herself. A few more trials like this, and my task is easy.'

CHAPTER II.

'THE MYSTERY OF THE PAST.'

MR. SAVILLE had taken matters easily, after that first burst of virtuous indignation at what he conceived his friend's baseness had subsided. He soon became himself a favourite with the earl, for Ardross, although scarcely entitled to be called intellectual, possessed intelligence far above the average of his fellow-wearers of strawberry leaves, and could especially appreciate talent in others. In addition to this, he was a rather advanced Liberal, and although his convictions would not carry him to the extent that Saville was accustomed to go, still he could not help but admire the unquestioned ability with which that gentleman, once fairly started on his favourite topics, would demonstrate the necessity of revolutionising England through every phase of what he forcibly termed her 'rotten and corrupt political and social system.'

Saville, moreover, was rendered easier in his mind as to the result of their renewed intimacy, after a few visits had enabled him, as he thought, to gauge Edith's character better. The conclusion which he arrived at was one which was a great compliment to Edith's powers of dissimulation. He considered her of too cold a nature to ever become a social sinner. Sin, he consistently argued, required a passionate temperament, and a rather fair share of intellect, to despise the after-consequences, and brave the contempt of those who were probably to the full as great offenders, save that they had not committed the unpardonable error of being found out. And thus misunderstanding her nature, and not rating her powers of mind at a high valuation, he felt sure that the hearth of the Earl of Ardross would never be visited with the scandal that he had at first feared was very imminent. Hammersley did his best, too, in order to throw him off the scent. He never let him know of his afternoon visits, and Saville was really now so absorbed in his new political work that he suffered his friend to go in and out without much questioning.

It was rather fortunate, though, that Saville happened to be out on that afternoon when he had extracted what seemed very like a confession from Edith ; for, in spite of his habitual self-command, there are some moments when the most self-possessed men would rather not meet the keen eyes of a friend who is in possession of their secret ; and it was very hard for Hammersley to keep his triumph to himself. He had seemed like a man groping in the dark all this time without Edith's love, and now that he could entertain some suspicion that that old love was not altogether gone, it appeared as if new light and life had opened all at once to him.

Saville and he met again at night, but by then he was sufficiently recovered to have successfully parried any suspicious inquiries his friend might have thought it his duty to institute ; for Saville was that rare anomaly in the present day, a thoroughly moral man. He despised the women who made a trade of

infamy too much to have any dealings with
them, and he would never have dreamt of
associating the idea of wrong with a woman
he loved.   It is an unusual virtue this same
morality in our present civilisation.   We talk
largely and unctuously in public about virtue
and honesty, and we send the wretch who
steals a loaf to feed his famishing children to
the treadmill; but we let some other little
dishonest transactions pass by with a lighter
punishment.   We deal very gently with the
criminal who steals a man's wife away from
him, and murders her in soul, if not in body.
An intelligent jury assess the injured husband's
feelings at a reasonable amount of damages;
and unless he feels prompted to take the law
in his own hand, and repair the wrong in the
short and deadly fashion that outraged nature
will sometimes suggest to sorely-tried men,
he must be content to be avenged according
to the institutions of his country; and an
admirable satire on the country itself nine-
tenths of those institutions are.

But a further surprise than any he had yet
dreamt of was in store for Hammersley.   The

next morning a letter was brought up to his bedside from Edith. He opened it eagerly, and read the following :—

'I send this letter to you because, after my weakness yesterday, some explanation can be fairly asked by you, and also because I would not that you should *see* me weak again. What I tell you now I am writing calmly and deliberately, although one so well versed in the ways and hypocrisies of the world as yourself can scarcely credit that I should record on paper such an avowal as I now make to you— that I, the wedded wife of another, love you with all my strength and heart. It is a candour which even those who pitied me would condemn as rash, and some men might revenge themselves by using it against me; but I have too much confidence in your honour to fear that, and I will tell you, simply and unaffectedly, the story of our estrangement, which may, perhaps, have hitherto seemed an enigma to you.

'I have little pride left in me now. Pride is for the happy, not the miserable, so I will spare myself no humiliation in what I have to tell you. I was always, from a child, jealous, and this morbid failing increased with my years till it became a disease threatening to blight, as it ultimately did, my whole existence. I was too proud to show it—I allowed it to eat into my heart and feed on it. All the while that I appeared the most indifferent, I was jealous, madly jealous, of every word and look of yours; I begrudged you every moment by the side of another, in my foolish dread that some one else's fascinations might lose me your love. You know yourself, a little, how I disliked Mrs. Jerningham. I daresay I had no reason, for I have grown older and wiser since then, and have learned to distrust and conquer many prejudices; but I could not help thinking then that you took more delight in her society than you would have done had you loved me as I wished, and thought I ought, to be loved.

'You must not be hard upon my vanity, Fred; you must recollect I was a spoiled child, and that I met with a deal of flattery on my introduction to society, which might

have turned many a wiser girl's head. I own
I was fond of admiration, and perhaps not so
scrupulous as I should have been in my manner
of winning it; but, flirt as you thought me,
my heart never wandered for an instant from
its old love; and, with a girl's folly, I fancied
that if you saw others admire me you might
like me better. I might have known by my
own feelings to you that this was a mistake;
but this riper wisdom only comes to us when
it is too late to repair the errors of which we
have been guilty.

'I disliked Mrs. Jerningham, as I have
said; in fact, I hated her, because I thought
you contrasted her with me to my dis-
advantage; but I was too proud to tell you
the cause of my dislike, and my anger and
jealousy at times drove me almost mad. I
was in one of these moods that night of the
ball. I had been coupling your names
together in my thoughts, till I would have
sacrificed everything for revenge. Unfortunately, all happened as if by concert to goad
me on. You did not come at the time I
expected you: that was enough of itself in

my then frame of mind to arouse my indignation, but what I heard afterwards seemed
to justify it. I shall now have to bring
another name into this letter—the name of a
man who owed his death to my thoughtless
folly, and over whom I have shed more bitter
and remorseful tears than any I ever wept,
except those I gave to the memory of our
buried love. Rochester was there that night.
It is no vanity on my part to say he loved
me ; his awful end proved that sufficiently.
He was naturally your rival, and in my
indignation I did not wait to analyse or distrust anything he told me to your prejudice.
He said that you had dined at the same house
with Mrs. Jerningham, and that afterwards
he had seen you in her box at the opera.
Fred, you can place yourself in my position
after this. You can fancy all I felt and
thought. At that moment I was not half,
but wholly, mad—outwardly calm as I
appeared. It was, in fact, the calmness of
desperation. You came—you were indignant
at my apparent indifference—afterwards I
could understand your indignation. I was

burning to heap you with a torrent of re-
proaches, only my pride forbade me to utter
them : I could only revenge myself by my
studied indifference. You felt it, and taxed
me with it, and then you know as well as
myself what followed.

'My pride had been too hurt to feel sorry
for the result for weeks to come. I kept
congratulating myself on my escape ; but, then,
in time, as I grew calmer, and could look at it
more dispassionately, I knew that I had been
to blame. I knew not whether I loved you
again; but if it was not love, you were always
in my thoughts. I remembered all our
childish days, all your words of tenderness,
till I could have almost wished for death to
banish memory from me for ever. *Then*, Fred,
could you have come over to me again, or
written to me, I would have returned to you,
and been a better girl than ever I was before ;
but my pride would not suffer me to make over-
tures, nor permit another to make them for me.

'I grew at last to bear my sorrow more
patiently, and to try and look upon you as
dead to me—as a link in my past life that had

dropped for ever out of the chain. And at this
time I was introduced to Lord Ardross. I did
not love him—at least not what I call love—
but I liked him, and I thought I could not
have you. You know the rest.

'And now I have told you my story, Fred;
I, the proud Edith Stewart, have laid my
heart bare before you, because I think that is
the least reparation I can offer for the injury
I have done you. Other atonement is impossible now. I know that which you—
which, perhaps, any other man so cruelly
wronged—would urge, but again I repeat, it
can never be. My own hand has wrought
the folly which has caused us such suffering ;
but, God be my witness, if you feel as a man,
I feel none the less as a woman. Dear as we
are to each other in heart, my marriage has
raised a gulf between us which you *must* not,
and I *will* not, cross. If I am traitress to my
husband's love, I will never pollute his honour
with my treachery.

'I ask you, is it not better, after this, we
should never cross each other's path again ? I
can be friends with you, with all my heart, if

you only wish for friendship, but I could not hear you plead, as I fear you would, for aught beyond. Spare my heart even the chance of a struggle between duty and sin. Fred, I know I have blighted your life, but the light has gone out of mine too. Will you help me not to add to that one miserable sin a yet more deadly crime ? '

He knew it at last. Her heart lay bare before him, and he, fool as he was, had never guessed at the depth of her love, and Saville, when he had gone to sound her, had come away as baffled. He sprung out of bed, and dressed himself hastily.

' No, no, Edith,' he muttered to himself, ' I have suffered too much myself to regard the sufferings of others. I will see her this afternoon, and if I do possess eloquence, it shall be exerted to the utmost. You robbed her from me, Lord Ardross ; it is only fair I take back my own.'

So he reasoned to himself, and so reason many others, yet, in nine cases out of ten, the world accounts them honourable men.

CHAPTER III.

'WHICH SHALL YIELD?

LORD ARDROSS and his wife were together in the room when Hammersley was announced. It is not often one is delighted with the spectacle of such conjugal harmony between fashionable couples. It certainly has its advantages, this high-bred indifference; for, if a woman has contracted an unhappy marriage—which, I should say, was the case ninety-nine times out of a hundred—she can easily live away from her husband, for society offers a home. It is true she may occasionally have to encounter her unpleasant better half, but every woman of *ton* knows how easy it is to avoid a husband in the fashionable world.

They are undoubtedly great philosophers, the upper ten, and unquestionably great in the art of following their own inclinations, without much attention to the breaches of morality or courtesy involved in so doing. In this respect the respectable middle classes are most behindhand. It is presumably from the fact that they are still fettered with the old-fashioned notions which obtained in those ancient days when virtue was new and attractive enough to be in fashion. A wife in this sphere is generally obliged to put up with her grievances, unless she seeks a remedy by seeking a lover, in which case her reputation is immediately besmirched by her scandalous sisters, and social extinction quickly follows. In the higher walks of life Mrs. Grundy is, fortunately, more merciful. She certainly lays the lash unsparingly on those unfortunates who sin openly and flagrantly; but for the little smothered peccadilloes, the sly flirtations with half-a-hundred lovers at a time, the dishonesty that pays its gambling debts and robs its tradesmen, the worthy old lady puts her whip in her pocket. Verily, my brethren, what filtrations of humbug society must go through before we shall show ourselves superior to the brutes in anything but cunning!

Some people are foolish enough to say that human nature is more powerful than everything. What a grand mistake it is. Fashion is the grand moving agent. Whether we wear the primitive garment of the untutored savage, or don the elegant habiliments that civilisation provides for us; whether Bill Sykes betrays his contempt for his wife by thrashing her till she can't stand, or the Marquis of Fitzboodle evinces *his* contempt for his aristocratic partner by the easy avoidance of her at home and abroad; whether we play at pitch and toss for halfpennies in the street, or stake our thousands over the dice in an aristocratic saloon; we are equally miserable slaves of the fashion which obtains in that station to which we are called, and which we are too cowardly not to follow, lest we seem to make ourselves singular, and provoke the ridicule of our fellows.

I have wandered far from the point where I left Hammersley entering the apartment of Lady Ardross; but when one enters on the wide field afforded by a view of the social anomalies of the day, the theme becomes practically inexhaustible.

Ardross welcomed his visitor heartily. There was a slight consciousness in Edith's manner—at least Hammersley fancied so—but this was not apparent to her husband. The latter's presence really rather took off the awkwardness of the meeting, which otherwise must have proved somewhat embarrassing. Englishmen and Englishwomen have a morbid dislike to own to emotion; and when a lady has informed a man that she loves him—especially when the confession of such love involves some sin, and possibly, also, some humiliation—even the easy nonchalant philosophy of the upper classes is sometimes powerless for a time to crush down natural instincts.

'How is Saville progressing in his new work?' asked Ardross presently. 'Does he expect it to be a success?'

'He is working at it unflaggingly,' returned Hammersley, 'and I believe, in his own mind, is very sanguine as to the result.'

'He will startle the aristocracy pretty considerably if he elaborates some of the arguments he has occasionally ventilated before us. They will think another Marat has arisen.'

'I think you do him injustice in comparing him with that almost monstrous production of an extraordinary time. Saville is rabid against abuses more than against those who commit them. I think if he were in power to organise the world to-morrow, there would be little bloodshed. He would seize the enemies of the people, but, after cutting their fangs, he would let them go free.'

' And whom do you call the enemies of the people ?' inquired Ardross. He was a Liberal, but one with an ' enlightened self-interest.'

' Ourselves,' laughed Hammersley, easily— ' the patrician order, the hereditary transmitters of blue blood, the professional conservators of the national wealth that should be diffused amongst the people, and not held by a class.'

' There is, undoubtedly, a most unequal distribution of wealth,' answered Ardross, thoughtfully ; ' but how can you remedy this by legislation? Don't you think such matters adjust themselves? What comes of revolutions? A few years of anarchy and bloodshed, and things flow quietly back into their old channels.'

'Revolution is in its infancy, as monarchy is in its dotage,' said Hammersley. 'From a few failures you infer their worthlessness. How many kings were beheaded and deposed to begin with, do you think, to enable monarchs to succeed each other peaceably as now? My dear fellow, in the moral and material world the tendency of all things is to find their level. The tendency of society is the same, and one day it will stand on the same basis. The lower strata will heave itself into the upper through one means, that is—education. When each man is thoroughly educated, he will permit no human creature to call him slave, but only fellow-creature.'

'Impossible!' cried Ardross, laughing. 'You are trying to regulate human beings and human passions, and energies and wills, as if they were inanimate puppets, or a perfect piece of mechanism. Trust me, Hammersley, society may grow wiser, more moral, more tolerant; but, as in the natural world there are hills and dales, mountains and valleys, so in the human there will be found their corresponding types, represented by higher and lower classes.'

'I won't dispute with you myself,' answered Hammersley, good-humouredly; 'I will set Saville on to you—a professor of the art.'

'So be it,' said Ardross, rising. 'Bring him to dinner with us to-night, and see which comes off conqueror—plain common sense, or ornamental imagination. I must ask you to excuse me now; you will amuse Edith in my absence.' And the earl departed.

'What a fool this man must be, if he loves her,' thought Hammersley to himself, 'to leave her alone with another man with such easy indifference.' It is almost needless to say he did Ardross wrong in this supposition. He was not a fool, but only unsuspicious; though I expect in these days an absence of suspicion goes far to establish a reputation for folly. It is in itself a testimony to our immorality, for it is the inevitable consequence of crime.

They were left alone for what must undoubtedly prove a painful interview. Edith was the first to speak.

'You have not regarded my advice that we should cross each other's path no more,' she said, unsteadily.

'I have not,' he answered, firmly. 'A criminal has the right to reply before he is condemned. You have not wholly banished me yet, and I may exercise my right.'

He paused a moment, expecting she might answer, but she spoke no word, only sat there with a weary, pained look on her face.

'Edith,' he continued, 'for many long and to me painful years I have endeavoured to learn your nature, and have been baffled in every attempt. You perplexed and eluded me. As the child I fancied I fathomed your love; as the woman I alternately believed and doubted it. God knows I do not wish to be harsh with you, unutterably as you have wrung my heart; but how much better for both our lives if you had shown your love plainly.'

'There is no need to reproach me with that now,' she said, quickly.

'Ah, Edith,' he answered, mournfully, 'it is easy to deprecate reproach, but we cannot put the past so easily from us. When the golden sunlight, the crimson glory of our morning, has departed, can we sit calmly down in the gloomy evening brought on by our own folly, and be always merciful when we think of the past beauty that has died out of our life?'

He spoke these words so inexpressibly tenderly, with that concentrated emotion which proclaims itself wrung from the very heart, that for the second time her woman's weakness conquered, and she wept.

'Oh, my darling,' he said, 'you weep now. Think how my heart has bled for you—for a woman's love compared to a man's is as the flame of a lamp to the scorching lava that scathes the sides of the volcanic mountain—for what weary years how I hungered and thirsted for you, even as Tantalus longed for the tempting fruit so near him; and yet, when, like him, I put forth my hand to gather the ripeness of the seasons, the fruit withered and crumbled at my touch. It is no vain rhapsody I pour upon your ears. I don't speak as a distraught poet or an amorous troubadour might have spoken in the days when compliment took the place of sincerity, and they were so alike that none could tell the true from the counterfeit; I speak to you as a sane, sober man, mad only so far as love has made him—for love, I hold it, is a delicious, and yet a cruel, madness. And I have been true to you, Edith. I have hated you at times, nay, even cursed your memory for the pain it brought, but my heart has never wandered to another : your image alone has been enshrined in it since I knew what love was ; and there it shall rest, without one sacrilegious intruder to disturb its peace, till I can feel and think no more.'

Could he have spoken like that in the old days, how differently had things gone then. Alas! I fear me, we are seldom eloquent, or sensible, till it is hopeless for us to reap benefit from being so.

'Oh Fred, darling, forgive me,' she said, sadly. 'I was blind to your love even as much as you were blind to mine. Would to

God that experience, which teaches us our errors, could point out a way to repair them. What would we not both give to forget?'

'That is useless,' he answered, quickly. 'Lethe's cup is for the careless and passionless; our natures are too deep for us to hope to escape the curse of memory. There is one way of repairing the error. Nay, do not shrink so guiltily, Edith—noble and true-hearted. women have done it before—have chosen to inflict a momentary wrong, rather than act a life-long lie. Is your love deep enough to do that?'

'My love,' she answered, and her eyes gleamed with unutterable passion as she spoke, 'is deep enough to peril all, but my honour forbids the sacrifice you demand.'

'Honour!' he repeated, scornfully, 'that is the word with which women jest and toy when they wish to drive their lovers mad— a word that helps us to say "no" gracefully, and shift the burden off our own shoulders on to those of the world. Hark you, Edith, you are not one of those weak women who set up conventionality as their god, and obey his behests with fanatic fervour.   Have you ever inquired in your own mind as to the real meaning of marriage?   Do you think the hollow mockeries that pass for rites in priest-ridden lands make a contract after God's own heart?   Tush! the savage chooses his mate more in accordance with divine laws than the Christian bridegroom, who buys his wife at the market price of the day.   Do you think the marriage that took you from me, your lawful husband in the eyes of One who, if He be a just God, must look with scorn on the cringing, greed-loving things that style themselves His ambassadors here, and joined you to a man who is but a representative of the Mammon to which this almost God-forgotten earth bows down with bated breath—a man whom, if you love me, you must hate, because he comes between us?   Are you still so much tinged with worldly cant and hypocrisy as to look upon this infamous contract as holy?'

'Hush! hush!' she cried wildly.   'For the sake of that God whose name you use to sanctify your specious reasoning spare me this.   If you have so little mercy, that you would slay my soul with your deadly sin, lay aside the hypocrisy that would paint vice virtue.   Do you think?' she exclaimed, hysterically, ' that I am, as you would express it, so God-forsaken, that I have altogether forgotten the difference? Do you think, if I were weak enough to do what your selfish passion prompts me, I could lift or reason away the brand of the adulteress?'

' Aye, it is ever so!' he said, bitterly. ' When a woman loves, everyone must be studied before her lover, has she wronged him ever so cruelly. What avail my weary years of suffering and broken-heartedness, if the feelings of others are spared laceration? It is the way of the world, I suppose : the true-hearted pay the penalty of a woman's folly— the undeserving reap the benefits of her conversion.'

She came and knelt down by his side, putting her arm round his neck in the old caressing way she had done when he had come to her for consolation in some childish grief.

' Oh, Fred, darling,' she said, softly and

sadly, 'I know what cause you have to hate me : I have wronged you so cruelly; but cannot you have a little pity for me ? I have suffered, darling, as well as you; I have suffered as only proud spirits can, because their pride makes them lock up their grief in their own breast, and refuses to summon to their aid that hysterical emotion which is such relief to weaker, or, perhaps, I should say, more womanly natures. You say a woman cannot love like a man. Oh, believe me, you are wrong. We are more single-hearted and purer in our love than you. We would die for you, but we would not demand from you such a costly sacrifice as you would demand from us. Woman's love seldom exacts, but man's love never spares.'

'You are a clever casuist, Lady Ardross,' he said, with a bitter, mocking laugh. 'You say our love is weaker than yours because it cannot wait and fume itself out against its own heart, as the prisoned bird flaps his wings against his cage till he breaks them. If that be true, then your love *is* stronger than ours ; and you prove it by sitting still and looking on, as the fanatic might look on his fellow-creature battling with the waters for life, and will not save him because he is not of his creed.'

'Unjust, unjust,' she murmured, sadly, 'as all men are when thwarted in things less dear to them than their passions. Oh, Fred,' she exclaimed, passionately, 'I will tell you what I thought I should never confess to mortal man : could I but take the full penalty of the sin on my own head, there is nothing I would not sacrifice for you. Name and reputation I would lay ungrudgingly at your feet, and the world's scorn should find ample compensation in your unfailing love.'

'Ah, why not do so now?' he asked, gently, stooping down till he felt her warm, fragrant breath upon his cheek. 'Come with me far away from the cursed tongues that would breathe shame upon the fugitive wife whom their poisonous teachings made such against her own heart. What need have we of friends? They would be but intruders upon our happiness. Oh, my peerless darling!—the glamour of whose beauty abides with me like

a deep, mysterious spell that warns me our
destinies are entwined, struggle against fate
as you will—be mine in deed, as you are in
heart ?'

His voice had sunk into a whisper; his lips
were pressed to hers in the mad intoxication
of passion, showering burning kisses, as in
hopes to melt the marble of her heart. Ah!
can our after dreams of love be interwoven
with such bright and gorgeous colours as
those which dawn upon us in the May morn
of life, when a woman's lips wet and warm
upon our own, a woman's eyes looking passionately into ours, we enter the gates of that
Eden, Love ? Verily, such brightness comes
not twice in our life.

She freed herself gently from that passionate
caress. 'Ah, no,' she said, tearfully; 'it cannot be. I must pay for the folly of loving
you; and you, darling,' she added, with a
sad smile, 'must pay for the folly of loving
me. We can never be more than friends.
Will you silence love—at least on your lips—
and be that ?'

'Friends!' he cried, passionately. 'That

means to see you the wife of another, and not begrudge him the possession of my treasure; to dream of the caresses he gives you, and steel myself to know they should be his and not mine; to play the hypocrite and masked traitor in your husband's home; to take him by the hand with a society smile, and wish to strike him dead at my feet. No, Edith, I am not actor enough for the *rôle* you assign me. Friends we cannot be.'

'Better so, perhaps,' she said, quietly. 'Then there is nothing for us but to part.'

'Part!' he cried, wildly, as the full force of that word for the second time struck upon him. 'Ah!' he muttered to himself, 'to part—that cannot be. I suppose it will be a little hard at first, but will get easier in time. Yes, Edith, since we can be nothing more, let us be friends.'

So they made the compact; but where man pleads and woman loves, can friendship last for ever?

CHAPTER IV.

'LOVE DEMANDS ANOTHER VICTIM.'

ANOTHER season commences, and the performers in the world of fashion gather again for a fresh rehearsal of the little drama that must be so wearily familiar to many of them. There is our old friend Lady Alicia to the front—a little more aged, of course, and a great deal more soured and cynical, since we last saw her, but energetic as ever. Verily, as long as there be eligible men about, and a clever maid to conceal the ravages which that republican, Time, inflicts even upon the aristocratic fair, Lady Alicia will not give up the matrimonial contest, be there never so many rivals in the field.

Mrs. Jerningham is also here, with a fresh poem in six cantos, which her critics find rather weaker than her previous productions; but she is an old stager now, and she laughs at reviewers. When you have once made a name, people will read you whatever trash or twaddle you put forth. Critics can make, but rarely unmake, a reputation—not, in this respect, very unlike the rest of mortals: we most of us find it easy to do, but the undoing thereof is sometimes terrible hard work, as I fancy must occur to many of those unfortunates who find themselves mulcted in breaches of promise and divorce courts, and compelled to 'take up' that little bill to which they put their name for a friend.

Among other changes, his place in the House of Lords, and in the peerage, knows the Right Honourable Hugh Childerton Hammersley, Baron Carnmore, no longer. That impatient waggoner, Death, has knocked at his door, and carried him off, with several of his legislative schemes for the amelioration of mankind imperfectly initiated. Natheless, never mind thy sudden summons, thou sturdy peer, thou hast done thy fellow-creatures some signal service in thy day; and if the grateful

incense of funeral orations pronounced by
hundreds can reach thee where thou art at
present established, thou shalt not complain
thou art unrewarded. Who is there would
not sooner be enshrined in the hearts of the
people than in the memory of kings?

It was no parting hard to bear between the
two. The dead man was proud of his son,
and ambitious that he should do well in the
world, as befitted the perpetuator of the house
of Hammersley; but his wife's death (strange,
too, that he died from the same cause) had
taken from him the capacity for much future
affection, and the son saw too little of him to
enjoy those intimate relations which used to
obtain somewhat in the old days between
parent and child, but which, I am afraid, are
becoming as much unfashionable in the present
day as many equally good institutions of the
past.

Neither Carnmore, as I must call him now,
nor the Ardrosses were yet in town. They
were scattered about somewhere in country
houses, waiting for a few weeks to throw them
together again in that vast meeting-place,

metropolitan society.   Some time had elapsed
since that day they instituted their compact
of friendship together, and up to the present
it had worked pretty well—pretty well, that
is to say, taking all the circumstances into
consideration. Perhaps, had they been moving
in pure London circles all this time—coteries
who constitute themselves minute historians
of every season—Ardross might have heard
some hints about his wife's former connection
with her cousin, which would have the effect
of making him a little less confiding; but
where 'ignorance is bliss,' &c.; and the earl
was as innocent as ever. I don't fancy Edith
much relished the prospect of the advancing
season.   There were sure to be many fascinating and beautiful women about, and sometimes she waxed a little doubtful of her power
over her lover's heart. Women may marry
themselves to spite their admirers, but they
don't like to see them committing a similar
folly.

Saville had come up from his brother's
house in Yorkshire rather early in the season,
in order to superintend the publication of his

new work; and having got his bantling fairly delivered over to the mercy of the reviewers and the public, he permitted himself to enter once more the society which, in the abstract, he despised.

He was one night present at a reception of Lady A——'s. There were several distinguished people there, among the rest Mrs. Jerningham, who presently beckoned him over to her side.

'Well, Mr. Saville,' she said, smilingly, 'you have been among strange lands and strange peoples; come and give me your opinion of them. Are our neighbours much better than ourselves, or tainted with the same vices, meannesses, and hypocrisies?'

'The world is but a large nation,' he said, gaily; 'the vices that one portion is destitute of it imports from its neighbour. Men and women seem to sell themselves for power and gold wherever civilisation and its attendant luxury obtain.'

'A bad report,' said Mrs. Jerningham, shaking her head with an amused smile, 'but scarcely, I fear, overcoloured. It seems that

even philosophers, like you and me, stand
aghast at the wickedness our investigations
reveal.   I think we must be content to let
the world wag on, and extract the little good
we may therefrom.'

'Sit down and fold our hands in the face of
the advancing tide,' answered Saville, good-
humouredly.   'Well, perhaps, that is the
easiest philosophy after all.   But, come, it is
your turn to become informer.   Tell me, what
has the precious crowd called society been
doing since my absence ? What fresh scandals
and new ambitions has it been amusing itself
with ?'

'Scandal has not been so rife lately,' said
the lady, gravely. 'Lord C—— eloped with
Mrs. M——; but that had been anticipated
for a long time, so that no one, except, probably, her husband, was surprised. Mr. D——
is ruined, and about to marry the widow of an
alderman—something in the grocery line
originally, I believe—in order to prop up his
fallen fortunes.   His family are naturally
shocked at such a plebeian alliance, but poor
D—— is too poor to have prejudices. As to

fresh ambitions, every mother hopes to win the Duke of L—— for her son-in-law, and the Duchess of G——'s receptions are the rage. I daresay many minor incidents have occurred, but these I have related are the gist of all the others.'

'Thanks,' answered Saville, gaily. 'I perceive the world of fashion goes on with no difference—not a new vice, and certainly not a fresh virtue. An encouraging prospect truly! The same philosophy with another application—the same religion with different idols.'

'But, stay!' interrupted Mrs. Jerningham, 'I have forgotten the most important item of all, particularly to an unmarried man: a new and unparalleled beauty has appeared last season in the shape of a Miss Maud Hilton. Her mother is a sister of the Earl of Ravenswood, and, it is whispered, had the honour to be considered a most beautiful woman by a no less distinguished judge than George the Fourth; so, you see, she comes with good credentials.'

'Ah, yes, I have heard of her,' answered

Saville, carelessly. 'Is she, in truth, as lovely as they describe ?'

'I call her simply perfect myself; but, perhaps, I may be rather partial, insomuch as she is a great friend of mine. However, you will shortly have an opportunity of becoming acquainted. She will be here to-night, and I will introduce you myself. Let me tell you that is no inconsiderable passport to her good graces.'

He thanked Mrs. Jerningham for her offer, and, perceiving an author of some note making his way to her, he relinquished his seat by her side. He had scarcely moved away when he encountered Melton.

That worthy gentleman was hale and hearty as ever, and as free from any *penchant* as a man could wish. I think, if you had placed him in the midst of the *houris*, he would have got tired of their fascinations in half-an-hour. His was a temperament suited for the mountains and the fresh, free fields : he could tolerate, but not enjoy, the atmosphere of saloons. Happy man! he did not know the meaning of love.

'What shall I say unto thee, most noble
Agrippa?' said Saville, good-humouredly. It
was the first time they had met, Melton having
been absent for a fortnight on some mysterious
proceedings connected with the forthcoming
struggle for the 'blue riband' of the turf.
'Who's going to win the Derby, Rocketer or
Suzerain?'

'Neither, in my opinion,' answered Melton,
confidently. 'If you want to back anything,
I can give you a better guess in three or four
weeks; but, at present, I rather trust to my
own stable to contain the winner.'

'I never bet,' said Saville; 'and, as a legislative reformer, I would utterly annihilate all
you gentlemen who stake your thousands on
the four-legged brutes; but since racing seems
a part of our national character, the least evil
I can wish you, as a principal aider and abettor
of the system, is that you may lose your money
to some one more deserving of it.'

'Thanks,' said Melton, laughing; 'your
kindness is overpowering; but let's talk about
other matters. Have you been introduced to
Maud Hilton yet?'

'Gad,' answered Saville, 'everyone seems to rave about this new beauty. She must be very superlative to justify all this enthusiasm.'

'So she is,' said Melton, emphatically. 'I used to think Edith Stewart well enough in her day, but this one eclipses everybody. She has broken no end of hearts already, and all apparently without any effort of her own; for her worst enemies can't call her a coquette.'

'A warrior who slays tens of thousands, and yet is not bloodthirsty!' answered Saville, incredulously—'a fashionable beauty and not a coquette! Truly, the century has produced an eighth wonder.'

'You see that foreigner with the dark moustachios talking to Lady Grenville?' asked Melton, indicating the direction where the pair were. 'That is a great admirer of hers, the Prince Ollinski. His title and wealth, of course, give him a good pull over other men, and he is tremendously persistent in his attentions.'

'And does the fair beauty seem to receive them favourably?'

'Well, one can hardly tell. The prince is

considered very clever, and she rather goes in for intellect ; but he has been dangling about such a long time, that it seems she can't quite make up her mind to accept him, and become an element in Russian society.'

They talked together on a few more subjects, and then separated, Saville waiting with some curiosity the appearance of the beauty who seemed credited with such power over men's hearts.

He had not to wait very long, for soon after Melton had moved from him she entered, leaning on the arm of her uncle, Lord Ravensworth, a tall. handsome man, with that easy patrician bearing which some of the old houses contrive to keep to themselves, as a contrast to the *parvenu* element that is daily invading their ranks. Saville was prepared to see something very beautiful, and he was not disappointed : Phidias could scarcely have sought a fairer inspiration for the Venus for whose model he ransacked all the diverse loveliness of Athens. Her features were simply faultless ; a world of thought and poetry lay revealed in her magnificent, earnest, blue eyes ; her wealth of glorious golden hair suited well her fair beauty ; with the symmetry of her figure neither artist nor sculptor could have found a fault ; and, resting over the clear beautiful features, hovered a saint-like repose, that made her resemble one of those Madonnas which the divine genius of the olden painters has bequeathed to our admiration.

Saville had seen many beauties in his time, at home and abroad, but he had never met anything approaching the spiritual loveliness of Maud Hilton. 'It is the face of an angel!' he muttered to himself, and hastened over to Mrs. Jerningham to remind her of her promise. She saw him approach, and smiled.

'Well,' she said, laughingly, 'are you smitten like the rest?'

'Hardened as I am by several seasons of fashionable life, I really feel quite enthusiastic. Will you introduce me at once?' he said.

'Nay, wait a little bit, most impatient admirer. Let her thin her ranks a little of the emptyheadedness and coxcombry that is sure to flutter around at the beginning, before

you intrude your sterling presence among the
common herd. I intend to present you with
a flourish of trumpets.'

And her advice was sound; for Maud
Hilton's sarcasm flashed rather unpleasantly
on the devoted heads of those admirers who
thought it the correct thing to appear in the
train of a celebrated beauty. Even the most
assured of those *fainéant* loungers of saloons
—men to whom a facility of conversation and
repartee is a necessary part of a first-rate
social education—found her cunning of fence
and deadly of tongue. If presumption had
to be extinguished with a sneer that stung
its victim like a keen rapier-thrust, none
were more capable of giving it than she.

How many people in every sphere, but
more especially in that of fashion, owe their
power to that rather feline quality of sarcasm
which makes them so dreaded by their fellows!
How we all detest such a man or woman, yet
how we propitiate them; how readily we take
up the laugh against our neighbour, yet all
the while quivering in agony at the thought
that the lash may next moment be turned

against ourselves! I suppose we fear sarcasm so much because we are conscious how much we deserve it, and there is some folly and some presumption that must be made to suffer before it can be cured of its offensiveness.

At last Maud was left by herself for a moment, and Mrs. Jerningham, taking advantage of the favourable lull in the ranks of her admirers, led the impatient Saville up to her.

'Maud, my dear,' she said, in her clear, ringing tones, 'let me make two distinguished people acquainted—let me introduce you to Mr. Saville. Beauty and intellect should be staunch allies. I know some of your sentiments, and some of his, and all I ask is, that you will not between you belabour too unmercifully the shoulders of that poor misguided animal, society.' And, with this laughing exordium, she moved away.

Maud smiled slightly at her friend's remark. 'You are known to me already, Mr. Saville,' she said, bending on him her earnest eyes, 'where they say a man's character is best gleaned—in your books. I have just finished your last one, and I cannot tell you how much I admire the principles I find there.'

Man of the world as he was, Saville felt a slight tinge of colour mount to his forehead as she said this, praise seemed so very sweet from those beautiful lips.

'I am flattered by such a disciple,' he said. 'Society, then, in worshipping you, as it seems to do, has reaped the usual reward of servility —contempt. I think it is not even worth that.'

'Society!' she echoed, contemptuously, and flushing slightly at the compliment he had implied. 'When I repeat that word to myself I long to be a man, that I could denounce it to the world.'

'Such a philosopher, after your first season!' he said, gaily, though not a little touched by her enthusiasm. 'You mistake, Miss Hilton: you have no need to be a man; your sentiments are too pure for eloquence to fail in their support. Suppose you turn author with me? We will write a joint diatribe—you shall lash the women, I the men.'

'Ah, Mr. Saville,' she said, with a smile,

'I wish it were possible ; but I fear you would
soon despise your literary coadjutor. No,'
she continued, earnestly ; 'I worship intellect
in others ; but I am afraid I must pay, not
receive, homage.'

'And yet you have an empire here great as
that which the man of genius can command,'
he said : 'his is over minds, yours over hearts.
It is difficult to say which is sweeter.'

'Hearts!' she repeated, scornfully. 'How
many hearts are there worth conquering *here*?
Is it an empire to hold one half where the
other is engrossed by a hundred petty meannesses and paltry idols? What true-minded
woman would sigh for such conquest?'

'And yet,' said Saville, gravely, 'even
among the falseness and frivolity, which you
describe too truly, there must be some precious
metal among the dross, some gold worth the
refining.'

'Perhaps so,' answered the impatient beauty;
'but what years we must waste in sifting the
base for the little pure left behind!'

They talked for some time on these and
other kindred subjects, and Saville took no

heed of the minutes, till he perceived the
Prince Ollinski advancing toward them ; and,
conscious that he had already engrossed the
attention of such a popular beauty a little too
long, he paid his adieux, and left the field free
for other admirers.

'We shall meet again, Mr. Saville,' she
said, graciously, as he prepared to depart—
'there is no escape from one another in that
very limited circle which calls itself the world
—and we shall have a large theme for future
conversation ; we have by no means exhausted
the immoralities of society yet.'

As Saville left he encountered Mrs. Jerningham, leaning on the arm of an *attaché* to
the Italian embassy. She quitted her escort
for an instant, and asked, in a low voice,
'Does she disappoint your expectations?'

It jarred on his somewhat sensitive nature
to hear her name discussed in that easy
manner, as if her fascinations were a thing
for her friends to take pride in, because of the
human hearts they could ensnare ; as if conquest were a woman's sole and legitimate
ambition.

'She is very beautiful,' he answered, gravely, 'and, better far than beauty, she has a noble nature. Maud Hilton, I should·say, is one of those women whose occasional advent redeems her class from utter worthlessness. Would there were many more of them.'

Mrs. Jerningham looked at him with a curious smile. 'Take care,' she said. 'You speak so earnestly in her praise, that I begin to fear you may some day swell the list of her victims. They are a goodly number already, I assure you; for Maud's blue eyes are very dangerous, if you look too often into them. Be prudent while there is time.'

He felt rather uneasy under her banter, good-humoured as it was. 'Never mind,' he said, with a rather forced laugh: 'if I have lived all these years to succumb to a hopeless infatuation at last, why, *kismet*, it is my destiny, I suppose; but, at any rate, I will not trouble my friends with my griefs : I will suffer, like the Spartan, in silence.'

'Easier said than done, if all tales be true,' laughed Mrs. Jerningham, gaily. 'We women can twist the wisest of you round our little

finger.' And, with the enunciation of this
general principle, she turned away, and resumed the arm of her *attaché* once more.

And Saville watched for a few moments the
woman whom she had just warned him
against. She was talking to the prince, a
tall, handsome man, with an intellectual,
though somewhat severe, countenance. It
was easy to see, by the stately deference and
courtesy he paid to her, that the charms of
his fair companion had made no small impression upon him. They were evidently discussing
some subject on which Maud had decided
opinions, for there was a look of animation in
her eyes, and a faint flush on her cheek, as
the beautiful lips were moving in answer to
what the prince had just said ; and, as Saville
looked there, all at once he felt a pang of
jealousy of the man who was sitting by the
side of that beautiful girl, who seemed to
appreciate his companionship so much.

He went home that night with Maud
Hilton's voice ringing in his ears, and Maud
Hilton's deep blue eyes, with their unfathom-
able earnestness, looking out of the darkness

into his own.   Truly, the shaft of the blind
archer, Love, had found him at last.   Was
it for peace or for misery he had been thus
smitten ?   And he remembered the letter of
Melton, which had come a year ago, describing
the advent of the new beauty, and how he had
read it through twice.   He wondered, as he
thought. of that, was there such a thing as
fate to bring two people together ?   Could it
be destined that he should be Maud Hilton's
love, and she the ideal that he had once
dimly sketched to the very woman who had
introduced him to her ?

CHAPTER V.

'A LOVE UNRETURNED.'

'THE sheen of Beauty's cheek, the light of
Beauty's eye.' My brethren, they have made
fools of the wisest of us since the world began.
Sages, statesmen, warriors, have all been
brought to a common level of folly by the
fascinations of woman. Verily, we must stuff
our ears, like the wary Ulysses, if we would
not hear the song of the sirens.

I wonder was it merely Maud Hilton's
beauty that made such wild work with
Saville's heart, or the glimpse of that noble
and pure nature underlying perfection of
feature and beauty of form; or, rather, was
it not the combination of both? Yes, he had
learnt, in what was but a few days, to love
passionately. The heart that had been sleep-

ing quietly for years, undisturbed by even one
of those boyish, romantic feelings which are
useful in taking off the first intensity of passion, had awoke suddenly in all the strength
and depth of a man's love.

And, yet, he knew Maud did not return it.
There was a friendly light in those earnest
eyes when she spoke to him, a friendly ease
in her manner when in his company; but he
felt a painful conviction that he could never
bring the blush of love upon that pure cheek,
the warmth of a lover's kiss upon those perfect
lips. Between those two souls there might be
sympathies, feelings, tastes in common, but
there never could be the link of passion. He
knew all this, and felt it bitterly, yet without
one thought of accusation against her. It was
not her fault that she could not love him.
When they parted day after day, night after
night, amid the meeting-places of society,
was it her fault that there was in her voice
no accent of passionate regret, in her hand no
lingering pressure, that could have told him
how dear was his presence, how painful his
departure? We sometimes learn to hate the

idol we once enshrined in our dearest thoughts, and the memory of her unworthiness will go far to banish the sting of disappointed love ; but, where those we have set our hearts upon cannot give us theirs, and yet are too gentle to wound save in the pain of that one direct refusal, how bitter is the love that loves in vain, and yet has no cause to hate !

Maud was no coquette. She was as free from that petty ambition of conquest as a woman could be. Those who had loved her to their own cost—and perhaps they were not few—had but themselves to blame for their folly. She disdained the arts of the professional flirt, as much as she despised the living targets against which the shafts of woman's vanity are directed. She had liked Saville. Amid a crowd of comparative nothings, it was a relief to meet two such exceptions to the common herd of pretentious folly or conceited genius as he and the Prince Ollinski; and she had been very friendly with them both, hardly heeding, till too late, that the friendship of a beautiful and fascinating woman is as dangerous, if not more so, than the wiles of the professed *intriguante*. Against the latter experience puts us on our guard ; in the former we suspect no evil.

But lately Saville's passion had been too unequivocally displayed to admit of doubt, and at the first revelation she had started, conscience-stricken, at the thought that she might have culpably fostered the illusion. The severest self-examination could not prove her guilty in her own eyes of what is termed 'encouragement,' but she blamed herself bitterly in allowing such friendship as had existed. She resolved to repair the mischief by the best means in her power. She accordingly avoided him as much as possible when they met, and if by chance they were thrown into a *tête-à-tête,* made it as short as lay within her power to do so without giving positive offence.

Saville was not slow to perceive this, nor to comprehend the motive. It was a further and convincing proof that to hope for her love was useless ; and then, so far had his passion mastered him, that he said to himself he would be content to win her only, and wait for her love to come. But there was one

thing to damp this resolve : he knew enough
of Maud Hilton to be almost sure that the
man she called her husband must have her
heart as well as her hand.   No disciple of
the doctrine of marriages of convenience was
the peerless beauty at whose feet a prince
was ready to throw his fortune ; and Saville,
in that strange metamorphosis of feeling
which is not uncommon to passionate love,
almost bewailed the fixity of those pure and
high principles which had first attracted him
to her.

He determined at length to know his fate,
whatever it might be ; and an opportunity
was not long wanting—it seldom is when
there is anything unpleasant to be commu-
nicated.   Lord Ravensworth gave a garden
party at his villa at Richmond, to which he
was invited.   Maud, of course, would be there,
and he would receive from her own lips his
sentence of hope or banishment.

In a social point of view his lordship's
garden party was an unequivocal success.
It was afterwards discovered that two pro-
posals and a fixed arrangement for the

elopement of a certain countess with a gentleman in the Guards, who had followed her very persistently for some time, were attributable to its influence. The perfection of well-dressed men and elegantly-attired women constituted a scene which would have sent an artist or the *Morning Post* into raptures. Lord Ravensworth belonged to the very upper crust of society, and his guests were consequently *la crême de la crême*—each individual almost alone a social power.

It was in one of those snug and out-of-the-way nooks to be found in every grounds designed for the gathering together of great multitudes of our fellow-creatures—I presume those who plan them fully recognise the exigencies of flirtation—that Saville met Miss Hilton, looking as beautiful as ever, but with a faint suspicion of *ennui* on her expressive features.

'You look somewhat wearied of this gay scene,' he said, with a slight smile.

'To tell the truth, I am a little,' she answered. 'We have nothing new, even in our pleasures, and one tires of *toujours perdrix*, you know.'

'And perhaps the queen is a little wearied also of receiving the homage of her subjects, who are gathered together in great force to-day?'

She flushed slightly at that remark, uttered lightly as it was.

'You credit me with a deal of power, Mr. Saville,' she answered, forcing a smile. 'I fear my influence is not so dangerous and deadly as you imagine. Like all flatterers, you exaggerate.'

'I can never exaggerate your power over men's hearts, Miss Hilton,' he said, quietly and earnestly.

She flushed uneasily again at that, and toyed restlessly with a bracelet on her arm. Somehow, she had a presentiment of what was coming.

He paused for a moment, and then the floodgates of his intense love were opened. 'The time has come when I must speak,' he said, passionately. 'Miss Hilton—Maud—may I call you by that name for this once? How can I exaggerate your power over men's hearts, when I know what it has done for mine? On the first night I saw you, I felt a curious, undefined fascination steal round my heart, environing it in its sweet, yet deadly, folds. Oh! would that I could have hushed my heart in that moment when I first learnt to distrust it; would that I could have fled for ever from the magic of your voice, the wondrous light of your earnest eyes; but I could not: I stayed, and drank deeper and deeper of the beauties that were poison to my own peace, till they made me what I am, and what I shall be, till death—your slave.'

He paused a moment from the intensity of his emotion, till he resumed:

'From my boyhood—from the days when I had first learned to think what love might be—I had dreamt of a pure idol, fashioned from a better than mortal clay. Among the daughters of society, all moulded after a coarse and common fashion, I sought in vain till I came to you. Oh! then I recognised at last the realisation of my boyish dreams. Tell me, and speak quickly—for it is cruelty to delay—have I found my idol at length only to see it shattered at my feet?'

Maud turned her head away an instant at that passionate appeal, while a look of intense pain swept over her features—the pain that a true-hearted woman must feel who listens to a love she cannot but respect, yet to which she knows there is no response in her own heart.

'Mr. Saville,' she said, falteringly, and the tears rose involuntarily to her eyes, 'believe me I had never dreamt of this till—till very lately, and then I did my best to avert it. What can I say to you now to soften the pain of the refusal I must give?'

'Say nothing,' he exclaimed, sorrowfully, 'except the bitter truth that you cannot love me.'

'Oh, why,' she cried, impetuously, 'were we women ever cursed with such a fatal gift as beauty—to woo us too often to our dishonour, or to something yet as deadly—the sacrifice of others' peace? I feel now like a murderess; for is it not your heart I have killed with my folly? Blind fool, that I was, not to foresee my own unhappy power!'

'Do not blame yourself,' he answered, in those deep, earnest tones that had vibrated to the core of a nation's heart. 'I, the greatest sufferer by our friendship, acquit you of guilt. Had yours been the arts of the practised coquette—had you been one sacrificing like those libels on their sex, your womanhood to your vanity, I would have hated you long ago. It is because you have so little in common with your sisters of society that I have loved you so passionately—that I love you still.'

Again the tears rose to Maud's eyes, touched deeply by this pure, intense love, which could outlive rejection thus.

'Oh, believe me,' she said, earnestly, 'if I could but accept your love I would hold that no woman ever made conquest of a nobler heart. I know that in rejecting it I am a heavy loser; but even were I to so far sacrifice my own feelings in the matter as to come to you because you ask me, I think I know you too well to fancy that you would not exact love for love.'

'I would wait,' he answered eagerly, while the prospect of that faint hope sent a thrill of fierce excitement through his pulse. 'I would adore you so that you *must* love me in return.'

She shook her head sadly.

'Indeed, it is not so. My nature is as wild and untamed in its love for liberty as that of the mountain eagle. I must be free to choose my own mate. Forgive me when I speak a harsh truth—you could never win my heart. The very calmness and sincerity of my friendship for you forbids the hope of love.'

'So be it, then,' he answered, gloomily. 'I am not one to whine and moan over my fate. I cannot say I will forget you—that were an idle promise ; but it shall not sap the strength of the manhood yet left to me, or deaden in me all other ambition. I will think of you as a bright and lofty star that I could not reach ; and, when you bless another man with the rich treasure of your love, my only prayer is that he shall be worthy of you.'

He seized her hand, imprinted on it one last, passionate kiss, and was gone—gone from the hubbub of fashionable voices, from the gaze of fashionable eyes—with a 'life-long hunger in his heart;' and Maud Hilton walked back to her uncle's guests, with a heavy heart and a troubled conscience, as she thought of the noble love that she was powerless to return.

CHAPTER VI.

'IN THE SEASON.'

IT wanted three weeks to the Derby, and the London season was in full swing; and Lord Carnmore, meditating on the subject, came to the conclusion that it was time to quit the pleasant quarters of his friend Sir Roland Vavasour, and betake himself to the metropolis. He was strengthened in this resolve by a letter he had received from Edith that morning, announcing their departure from where they were staying. They corresponded, these two, very frequently, but nothing save exceedingly decorous epistles passed between them, such as might be between people who had been brought up from childhood together, and regarded each other with a pure brotherly and sisterly affec-

tion. She invariably showed his letters to her
husband, and a more suspicious man than he
could not have discerned much harm in them.

Time had changed Carnmore a little, too :
it had turned him into an author. He had
written some poems, rather wild and weird
productions, yet bearing unquestionably the
stamp of genius ; and the public and the
critics, rather in want of a new sensation, had
accorded him the fame of a successful poet.
I am not sure whether the fresh ambition
stirred in him by the success of this appeal to
' men, gods, and columns,' had not taken off a
little of the absorbing interest of his love. I
am afraid the wisest of us like to *pose* before
the world, and are pleased if it approves of
our performance ; but, still, he was not disposed to make ambition his sole mistress : so,
three days after the reception of Edith's letter
found him speeding by an express train to the
capital.

Things were going on much the same as
ever in the fashionable world ; at least, so he
learned from the gossip of the clubs, whither
he had betaken himself to pick up the news.

He and Melton were lounging in the smoking-room of one of the most aristocratic of these bachelor retreats a night or two after his arrival in town. To them presently entered others of the male *beau-monde.*

'Tell you what it is, Melton,' said Harry Verney of the Guards, a tall, good-looking, blonde man, well-born and well-connected enough, but one on whom the manœuvring guild looked rather askance—he was too encumbered with debt to be good for anything except flirtation—'if you have any real designs on Maud Hilton, you had better go in at once. Ollinski is making the running fearfully, and a prince is a tempting prize for our weak-minded maidens.'

'Thank you,' answered Melton, easily. 'I thought everybody could see I was not *épris* in that quarter.'

'Hear him, the cold-blooded Stoic!' exclaimed Verney, indignantly. 'Not *épris*, he says, with all the coolness imaginable, as if he were talking of a marble statue or the draped figure in a tailor's window. Why, man, who *could* help raving on such a divinity?' '

'Why don't you go in for her yourself,
then ?' asked Melton.

'That's a sensible question to ask a man
whose liabilities have long ago got beyond
the reach of ordinary computation,' answered
Verney, with a comical shrug of his shoulders.
'A man in my impoverished condition can
only flirt with married women and rich widows,
who have nobody to take care of them. If I
were to commence serious relations with any
eligible maiden, the whole band of London
mothers would unite in preparing a bull for
my excommunication from every drawing-room
where they held sway.'

'It is the fitting penalty for such graceless
scamps as you,' said Carnmore, with assumed
seriousness ; 'and, yet, you think yourself very
hardly used to find that no mother will allow
you to offer the dregs of a worthless life to a
pure-minded girl.'

'You pitch it rather too strong about pure-
mindedness,' answered Verney, with a laugh.
'I think there is a great absence of that
quality in the worldly young ladies of the
present day. Bad as we are, I don't think

we are worse for men than they are for women.'

'That's not such a bad remark for you, Verney,' said that veteran man of the world, comparatively young as he was in years, the Honourable Harry Desmond: 'you are improving in social knowledge.'

'I know this fact, and, deeply as I deplore it, it nevertheless remains,' said Verney, surveying the assembled company with an amusing expression of plaintiveness on his good-natured face—'if society won't forgive a man his little youthful indiscretions, and won't allow him to sow his wild oats, no matter how much he wants to, why, I say, in such a case, since it refuses him any one of its daughters to work his conversion, when he does want to take a wife he must, unfortunately, take some one else's.'

There was a general roar, of course, at this easy philosophy of the young scapegrace, and Carnmore said, with a smile—

'That will, no doubt, be your case, Verney, and we shall yet live to see you in the

Divorce Court, mulcted to the tune of several hundreds.'

'It's very hard to keep out of it in fashionable circles, when there are so many women wanting to run away from their husbands.' And, with this parting shot, Mr. Verney departed.

'Rum fellow that,' remarked the Honourable Mr. Desmond, as soon as he was out of hearing; 'clever in his way, but not much troubled with principle, I fancy; and I generally find that no man succeeds in life without a little of that commodity.'

'To profess it is quite enough. The Joseph Surfaces of real life get on better than the Charles's, I fancy, though not half so good at bottom; and, in real life, they have the advantage of seldom being found out,' said Carnmore, with an emphasis that was not lost upon his listener, for Mr. Desmond, although the first to discover want of principle in his friends, was not particularly noted for it himself.

'But we have wandered far from the main question,' interposed Viscount Wraxall, son of the Earl of Debenham, and a noted beauty man. 'Why is our friend Melton so obdurate to female charms?'

'Because it is "my nature to," I suppose,' laughed the addressed.

'I don't believe he has been moved a particle by one of our beauties since his first season,' continued his lordship, with as much energy as his lazy disposition and reputation for *ton* would permit him to assume.

'I can change your belief into certainty,' answered Melton, coolly: 'I never *have* been "moved," as you express it.'

'You are a d——d queer fellow, then,' said Wraxall, to whom the subject of his friend's obduracy seemed to furnish matter for grave reflection. 'Nearly all of us get bit in our first youth. We have been so unaccustomed to the sight of a respectable-looking woman, either at the public schools or the 'Varsities, where we pass our early life, that when we meet them, tricked out in gorgeous laces and jewels, we regard them as divinities, and fall down and worship.'

'That is, until we find how very mortal they

are,' commented Carnmore, with a slight sneer.

'The awakening from the ideal is very painful, I confess,' returned Wraxall, pathetically. 'If a man wants to be a believer in pure and unsullied womanhood, he should die in the first week of his first season—the illusion does not last longer.'

'You admit this, and yet wonder that I am philosopher enough to despise what you condemn yourself?' asked Melton.

'My dear fellow,' replied his lordship, easily, 'it is no hard matter to despise, but it is sometimes exceedingly painful to renounce what we despise. Were it not so, I take it, we should be a perfect people. It is a case of nature struggling against conviction; and in all these little contests I have generally found nature get the best of it.' And having delivered himself of these sentiments, Wraxall looked round complacently, evidently deeply imbued with the notion that he had edified his listeners to a considerable extent.

'And I suppose it is to this inherent weakness of our human composition that we may attribute Lord Wraxall's openly-displayed

penchant for the Countess of Veriphast?' said
Carnmore, quietly.

His lordship so far forgot his fashionable
training as to colour slightly.

'Let us discuss principles, not persons,' he
said, gaily. '*Affaires de cœur* are the common property of one's friends when one's
back is turned—that's a matter of course, and
nobody blames the exercise of this privilege
to say what they like of us; but at least have
the decency to wait till we *are* gone.'

'I humbly apologise for my sin against
the proprieties of scandal,' answered Carnmore, with assumed contrition. 'As for our
friend Melton, depend upon it, he will not
keep hard-hearted for ever. The day will
come when he shall become a hopeless slave
to bright eyes and ruby lips. Well for him,
my masters, if in that day he shall not have
to cry " *Væ victis.*" '

'Love cometh soon or late,' quoth Wraxall,
sententiously. 'When men are attacked with
the disease late in life, they generally become
hopeless idiots. Better to have it while our
strength and constitution are at their best.'

'Poor Rochester had it young,' remarked another of the company; 'but his constitution didn't seem proof. I suppose there is no doubt Edith Stewart was at the bottom of his unhappy end?'

Wraxall shot a warning glance at the speaker, who had forgotten, in his eagerness to add to the stock of conversation, that Edith Stewart's cousin was present.

'Poor Neddy Rochester!' he said, contem-platively. 'He was a good man and a true compared to some we see nowadays; but his was not, after all, such an unjust retribution. He had broken many hearts in his time, with as little compunction as if his victims had been wax models, instead of human anatomy and emotion.'

Carnmore and Melton rose to go; they were both bound for the Countess of A——'s. '*Au revoir*,' said the former, gaily, as they turned to depart. 'Don't be too severe upon us when we are gone; we leave our reputations in your hands—deal mercifully with them, if you can.'

'My parting advice to you, Carnmore, is to

go in for Maud Hilton. I can promise you, you will be enchanted by her beauty; and, as she affects intellect and all that kind of thing, I shouldn't be surprised if she took wonderfully to you. Only you had better be sharp : you heard what Verney said to-night : Ollinski is running her very closely; but I don't despair if you are quick about it. Englishmen beat Russians at Sebastopol, and . I don't see why they shouldn't beat them in love.'

'I will consider your advice after I have seen the young lady; at present, I am only acquainted with her by reputation.'

'I want to call at Saville's,' said Carnmore, as they descended the steps of the club; 'there is plenty of time for the countess yet.' So the friends separated, Carnmore taking a hansom to Saville's lodgings.

He was surrounded by books and papers when Carnmore entered, but rose cordially to meet him.

'Welcome to London again,' he said, heartily; 'it seems centuries since I saw you last.'

'Thanks; you are very complimentary,' answered Carnmore. 'I, too, have languished for a congenial mind. But I am disturbing you, perhaps, at an unseasonable time.'

'Not at all,' he said, cordially. 'I was only diving, for the hundredth time, into the history of that stupendous social drama, the French Revolution, and, in reality, I shall be glad to give my brains a little rest. What news do you bring from the country?'

'None,' answered Carnmore, laughing, 'except that the agricultural population is ground down as much as ever, and that the landlords labour under the delusion that they do their duty.'

'Eight shillings a week a respectable income, and twelve affording positive luxury—that's the general view the landlords take of their position,' said Saville, sarcastically. 'Well, I suppose they took matters as easily as that in France, before the upheaving of the masses crumbled their rotten power into the dust.'

'And I suppose we will see the same thing in England some day—revolution or its equivalent,' answered Carnmore. 'By-the-way,' he added, 'Melton tells me he has seldom met you lately. How is that? Have you elected to play the part of Timon?'

'I don't go out so much now,' said Saville, with a faint and rather embarrassed smile. 'I have grown somewhat weary of society by now.'

'Yet, you ought to mix in it, were it only to discover that ideal you have painted to me so eloquently at times.'

'Ah!' he answered, curtly, 'I fear there is nothing approaching my standard in the conventional world.'

'Talking of women,' said Carnmore—'have you seen this new beauty everyone is raving about—Maud Hilton?'

'Yes, I have seen her,' he answered, briefly. How that name, carelessly uttered by his friend's lips, thrilled to his heart's core.

'And what is your opinion—is she a "perfect woman, nobly planned," &c., &c., or very sublunary, like the rest of us?'

'She is very beautiful,' he answered, quietly, 'and vastly superior, as far as I can judge, in depth of sentiment and emotion, to her sisters of society. The rest you must decide for yourself.'

'But, still, for all her evident superiority, not answering to your ideal?' said Carnmore, interrogatively.

'No, she does not realise my ideal,' he said, rather indistinctly. In the first bitter moments of his deep sorrow he had longed to pour forth the history of his unhappy love into some sympathetic ear; but, now that he had grown calmer and better able to bear his disappointment, his sorrow seemed too sacred to be profaned by even the sympathy of another. He hastened now to change the conversation.

'And how fares the empress of your heart, Lady Ardross—does the friendly compact still hold good?' he asked.

'Oh, yes,' answered Carnmore, with a slight tinge of bitterness in his tone—'we play the brother and sister to perfection; we write charming little notes on the changes of the weather, and other equally interesting subjects; we banish love from our eyes, and from our lips; in short, we are great hypocrites, but we manage to preserve our virtue;

which, of course, is a great thing, is it not?'

Saville smiled slightly. 'You know my opinion already,' he said.

They talked for some time on various topics. It was so long since they had seen each other, and events had been so numerous and stirring, that an hour passed away almost imperceptibly. At last Carnmore rose to go.

'I am bidden to the Countess of A——'s,' he said, 'and, as her ladyship of Ardross will be there, I must needs pay my friendly homage.'

'I am going to the House,' answered Saville, rising with his friend; 'and as Lady A——'s is close, we can walk together.'

As they just turned out of his lodgings a carriage dashed by them. Carnmore felt a pressure of his friend's arm.

'That was Maud Hilton inside, with her mother,' he said. Carnmore hastily glanced in the direction of the retreating carriage, but it was too late. She had seen Saville in their rapid progress, and a look of pain stole over her calm, beautiful face, as she leaned back beside her mother, and murmured to herself, 'Poor fellow! I wonder if he has forgotten me.'

'It is always my luck!' cried Carnmore, in a tone of vexation. 'I have heard so much about this wonderful girl since I have been in town, that I would have given anything to see her to-night.'

'Don't chafe at that,' said Saville—and his friend did not notice at the time that he spoke more earnestly than his wont—'you will be sure to see her soon. If all tales be true, many would give anything if they never had met her.'

'I must take care not to fall a victim myself, after such a dreadful description,' said Carnmore, with a laugh. 'Perhaps I am not so badly off, after all: if it had not been Edith Stewart, it might have been Maud Hilton.'

They parted soon after, Saville to the House, Carnmore to the countess's. As the latter walked along, he could not help thinking that there was a certain undefinable change had taken place in his friend—a peculiar, subdued, and earnest air which he had never observed before.

'Something peculiar, though I can't quite make out what it is,' he muttered to himself. 'He certainly can't have fallen in love, or he would have told me of it.' Wise judges are we of our friends, you see!

CHAPTER VII.

'FIRST IMPRESSIONS.'

IT was Lady Ardross's first season since her marriage, and many of her old admirers flocked round her immediately; for your man of fashion thinks there is nothing confers greater social distinction among his fellows than a *liaison* with a married woman. But those sanguine mortals who based their expectations on the maxim, 'Once a flirt, always a flirt,' found themselves grievously disappointed. Rumours concerning the married couple had, of course, got about, and reached the ears of those interested; but scarcely anyone was prepared for the great change matrimony had wrought in Edith. In the days when her success as a fashionable beauty had turned her into a coquette, she had been noted for her powers of sarcasm—powers which more than one luckless cavalier had drawn upon his devoted head ; but this was now replaced by a haughty indifference, which was infinitely more galling to those to whom she chose to display it. Dislike is better to bear than contempt. No man cares to be considered so insignificant that he cannot make an enemy.

The Marquis of Courtown, who had been a very faithful, and somewhat favoured, follower of Edith's in her maiden days, had not been without hopes that he might establish himself ultimately on a more familiar footing, but her indifferent demeanour soon convinced him that his chance was hopeless. He had been exerting himself to his very best one night, but all to no purpose. Edith had so completely ignored any claim upon her that his former acquaintance might lead him to prefer, that his lordship—not at any time blessed with a particularly sweet temper— waxed somewhat wroth, after the fashion of men who are disappointed in their designs on their friends' wives.

'I should hardly recognise you,' he said,

gnawing savagely at the amber moustache that was kind enough to afford a little obscurity to the sensual look of his patrician mouth. 'You used to be a flirt of the first water in the old days, and now '—— A shrug of the shoulders finished the sentence, for his lordship was not blessed with eloquence, even where his own passions were concerned.

'I have renounced flirting altogether,' answered Edith, quietly.

The marquis relieved his vexation by another mastication of his moustache. 'I don't put much faith in such sudden conversions,' he said, with a sneer; 'a flirt is born, not made; and, for my part, I don't see much harm in the pastime.'

Edith turned round, and looked the young nobleman steadily in the face. He involuntarily lowered his eyes before the cool, contemptuous expression in her own.

'There is no harm in flirtation, Lord Courtown, when it is only meant as such,' she answered, in a cold, clear voice. 'It has a bad name simply because some fashionable gentlemen have looked upon it as a certain means to a certain end ; otherwise it is, as you say, a sufficiently harmless pastime for vain women, and men who are silly enough to pamper their vanity.'

The marquis turned a furious red at this denunciation of ' arts which caused himself to rise,' and after that evening he contrived to give Lady Ardross a very wide berth. The earl, to whom Edith afterwards gave a recital of this adventure, waxed enthusiastic in his admiration at his wife's easy fashion of putting down what, in the privacy of their own conversation, he denounced as a ' damnation puppy.'

Lord Courtown she had, of course, openly offended by that remark ; but she contrived to say several unpleasant things in a quieter, but scarcely less emphatic, fashion, to the other coxcombs, whose homage now seemed to her an insult; and the end of it was that the Countess of Ardross waxed somewhat unpopular. In the true sense of the term, she had never been popular : her wondrous beauty had attracted numerous admirers, and some victims, but not one of either class could have said that Edith Stewart was in herself a lovable girl, or worth the sacrifice implied in an unrequited affection.

Ardross, naturally, was secretly delighted at the cold reception his wife afforded to her old admirers, and which, of course, contrived to get, by some circuitous route, to his ears. His knowledge of London society was sufficient to have prepared him for the toleration of a certain amount of flirtation on the part of the ' partner of his bosom,' and he was agreeably disappointed. Perhaps he would not have discovered such cause for self-congratulation had he fathomed the real reason of Edith's indifference—that her absorbing passion for one man rendered the language or pretence of love intolerable from another.

I think that at this period Carnmore's own feelings towards his cousin must have changed somewhat. In all dangerous maladies we are accustomed to the spectacle of sudden rallies and relapses in the suffering patient; and love, I presume, is like most other diseases in this respect—that the victims occasionally manifest symptoms of convalescence, or, at least, amendment.

They had met cordially and friendly, and he had visited her as frequently as his relationship with her, and friendship with her husband, permitted ; but he began to find the *rôle* he had promised to assume terribly irksome. His old sense of the deep wrong she had done him increased on him more and more, as the apparently matter-of-fact way in which she regarded their relations forced itself upon him ; and, although he scrupulously avoided— more, perhaps, from pride than any other influence—tabling the forbidden subject again to her, his bitterness would betray itself sufficiently to make her very miserable after he had gone.

It was a hard struggle for her, poor child ! harder than he could wot of—that contest between passionate love and the stern voice of duty. I think men, even the best of them, are terribly unjust to women. They are the first to tempt them to fall, but they are also the first to suspect their faith for ever after. The world cries loudly against the woman who breaks her social ties for another love; but I do not envy her her life with her seducer.

It was not long before Carnmore obtained an introduction to Maud Hilton. It is almost needless to say that had the question been asked by another, nay, had he even at first put it to himself, 'Can I love again?' he would have unhesitatingly answered 'No.' But man is only man, and the love of beauty is a factor in his composition. The seraphic loveliness of Maud was peculiarly congenial to one who had, long ago, imagined his ideal of a woman as something a little lower than the angels. Her fascination lay in what Saville had told her on that memorable afternoon—her utter dissimilarity to the rest of her sisters of society : her sympathies were so keen, her sentiments so pure. As a man, she would have identified herself with a great cause, or a great principle ; as a woman, she could only hope to minister to the genius of another. At present, with all her pure womanhood, she was discontented, and, at times, disdainful. It scarcely needed a philosopher to tell that her happiness, like that of even some of the most worthless of her sex, to be rendered complete, needed the wand of the great magician, Love.

She knew Carnmore's poems well. The weird and romantic spirit that breathed through them harmonised well with her own. She was a strange mixture of coldness and warmth : she was romantic, but of a romance different to ordinarily enthusiastic people—it was pure, not sensuous ; she could have loved to the death, but she was free from voluptuousness, or, rather, it was the difference between love and passion—the one a divine, the other an earthly, emotion—which made her a perfect woman, yet so superior to most of those with whom she shared her sex.

Carnmore had met her a few times at various houses, but had enjoyed few opportunities of testing whether her mind and nature were equal to her beauty; but one night, at a ball given by one of the leaders of fashion, he presumed sufficiently on their slight acquaintance to ask for a dance.

She bowed her head courteously to his

request, and handed him her card to inscribe his name on. While he was occupied in this she said—

'I should have thought a poet, who can denounce frivolity in such strong language, would have been superior to a quadrille.'

He handed the card back, and replied, with a slight smile—

'The old story, Miss Hilton : the greatest philosophers in public are but weak mortals in private. We preach, but we fail in our own practice.'

'And how can you expect to regenerate the world if you don't set a good example ? Man is an imitative animal, you know.'

'Rather, how can you expect us to cure frivolity when it is an element of human nature ? '

'By making it unfashionable,' replied Miss Hilton, sharply.

'Excuse me,' answered Carnmore ; 'but you mistake the disease, and, consequently, its cure. If you want to make men sensible and give them noble ambitions, there is but one means, and that is education.'

'I say give them freedom, and the rest will follow,' said Maud.

'Ah!' replied Carnmore. 'You hold the same opinion as my friend Saville. You have met him, I think.'

'I know Mr. Saville very well,' answered Miss Hilton. She had sufficient self-command to conceal her emotion at the mention of that name from the eyes that were looking intently at her. 'But I have not seen him at all lately. I suppose his affection for the un-emancipated portion of his fellow-creatures has led him to renounce society for a time.'

'I don't think he derives much pleasure from our constantly recurring gatherings. I don't presume any philosopher would be favourably impressed with the various shades of human weakness, meanness, or ambition that are exhibited in such.'

'You are right,' she answered emphatically, 'very right.'

'And yet,' said Carnmore, with a smile, 'much as he despised society in general, he gave a most flattering description of one of its greatest ornaments—to wit, yourself.'

This time Maud Hilton's usual self-control
did not stand her in good stead. A faint blush
rose to her cheek, and it was a second or two
before she recovered herself sufficiently to ask,
'As you have gone so far, you must needs
satisfy my curiosity in full, and tell me precisely how he described me.'

'Were it only in the interests of morality,
I fear I must refrain,' said Carnmore, laugh-
ingly. 'Even a successful beauty like Miss
Hilton may receive too many compliments.'

'But I know Mr. Saville so well,' she urged,
'I am sure, if he spoke of me, it would be in
all sincerity. He is not one to adopt the
language of compliment for compliment's
sake.'

'Oh, the casuistry of women!' answered
Carnmore, with a smile. 'Well, then, Miss
Hilton, since it must be, I will betray my
friend's confidence. Having heard of you so
much, I was naturally anxious to ascertain
the nature of your claims to so much admiration, and I thought I could apply to no better
person than Saville; because, in the first
place, I knew him to be a good judge of

character, and, secondly, because I had hitherto found him impervious to the fascinations of beauty, and always more ready to condemn than praise. So I asked him, and his reply was—don't I tantalise you very much with my delay ?'

'Dreadfully,' answered Maud. 'Pray go on a little faster.'

'Well, his reply was—I give it you almost verbatim—that you were very beautiful, and, in point of character and sentiment, infinitely superior to the women of society by whom you were surrounded.'

She was silent for a moment, and then she answered, very earnestly—'I thank Mr. Saville for his good opinion, which, I fear, is far beyond my merits ; but I can bear equally favourable testimony to him. He is as superior to average mankind as I am, in his estimation, better than ordinary womankind.'

Her momentary enthusiasm had made her look very beautiful, and Carnmore's face expressed his admiration, as he said—

' My acquaintance with you is very slight, and what I am about to say might be considered by some as impertinent, but I show my belief in your superiority to ordinary women by despising the conventionality which is a part of ordinary women's existence. I know your reputation in society; I know the flattery and admiration—some of it very false, some very true—which you must meet with; and, if you have strength of mind and singleness of heart sufficient to enable you to appreciate them at their real worth, I can only say that you more than justify my friend's description.'

'There is no impertinence in your frankness, Lord Carnmore,' she said, quickly; 'for,' she added, with a slight blush, 'you are not such a new acquaintance of mine as you suppose. Your poems have formed part of my favourite reading, and although, conventionally speaking, strangers, I fancy there is always some link between genius and those who appreciate it.'

It was Carnmore's turn to feel flattered, and he was hastening to express his gratification in her admiration, when she stopped him with a pretty gesture of her hand.

' Nay, nay,' she said, with a slight smile, ' no compliments. Those may do well enough for *society*; we, who are above it, should practise sincerity. When I say that the perusal of your poems has afforded me pleasure, I only speak the truth. I am not one of those young ladies who flatter a " lion," in order to gain for themselves the reputation of cleverness.'

' I should like to know your victims,' he said, gravely. ' They must be foemen worthy of your steel, I hope. Coxcombry and foppery are certainly not worth your conquering.'

' I trust I have no victims, as you call them, Lord Carnmore,' she answered, seriously. ' I despise the false arts of the coquette, even more than I compassionate the folly that suffers itself to be lured by them. Love is too serious a thing to be sacrificed to a woman's love of power ; and my remorse would be deep if I had pained a human heart through mere heedlessness.'

Carnmore's admiration for the beautiful girl beside him was thoroughly genuine. She had spoken the sentiments which he had put into the mouth of his ideal in the dreamy days of youth. Here, at last, was a woman whose deep and earnest spirit was congenial to his own.

'Miss Hilton,' he said, in a tone of real feeling, 'I can more than endorse Saville's opinion of you, from my brief experience to-night. The heart for which you give yours in exchange should be indeed a noble one.'

At that moment the Prince Ollinski approached, and their *tête-à-tête* was ended. Carnmore observed with some curiosity the man whom common rumour assigned as her future husband; but the little he could gather from the brief scrutiny did not impress him with the idea that he was the kind of man to whom Maud could give her heart, although one from whom it was impossible to withhold her respect. After all, love will be satisfied in these little matters.

As he sat late that night consuming the cigar in which he generally indulged before going to bed, he could not help contrasting Edith with Maud. They were similar in this respect, that the one had been, the other was, a reigning beauty, with apparently the same amount of power. But what an immense difference between the two natures! And he sighed as he thought how well it might have been could Edith have more resembled her rival. There was something so spiritual, so angel-like, about Maud, that love for her would have rather resembled a worship than a passion —the worship of goodness, and gentleness, and purity. Edith had been loved for her beauty and waywardness. Her empire was over the heart alone; reason would have rejected her sovereignty. I wonder which is the idol to whom men bend the knee most, the one around whom they are almost afraid to throw their arms lest the contact sully its purity, or that which they clasp in the feverish excitement of an earth-born, earth-stained passion.

And Maud, as she sought her couch that night, thought of the three men whom she had alone found superior to the pettiness of the rest—Saville, Ollinski, and Carnmore. In the first she recognised the noblest nature, perhaps, of them all; but the tenderness of love he was powerless to awaken. She knew enough of the prince to doubt his ever moving her heart deeply; and she had seen the other but a few times, and conversed with him for any length only that night, yet his image seemed to dwell longer with her than the others, staying with her till sleep came to banish all earthly thoughts for a brief while.

CHAPTER VIII.

'A RIVAL IN THE FIELD.'

EDITH, Countess of Ardross, sat alone in the luxurious apartment in which she was accustomed to receive her visitors. Young, rich, high-born, and beautiful, what would not many have given for one-half of her advantages? How eagerly would many of her own sphere have clutched at the coronet she took so little pride in wearing! Yet, she sat there, surrounded on all sides by the evidences of luxury, the wife of a fond and indulgent husband, with a strange, restless discontent on her fair, proud face.

It had come home to her at last, that life-long remorse which she had purchased for the gratification of a moment's pride! The chains in which she had voluntarily manacled herself

were beginning to gall and bruise her sorely.
The means by which she had hoped to revenge
her insulted dignity upon her lover had
answered their end, but at what a price!—
at nothing less than the cost of her own
happiness!

And there was one thing that was gnawing
at her heart almost more bitterly than her
disappointed love, and that was the wrong
she had done to the man who had trusted in
her faith so implicitly, who believed in her so
fully still, unsuspecting of the guilty passion
that consumed her soul. Imbued with much
of the world's easy morality in trifling errors,
she had not yet acquired that laxity of
principle which could lead her to gloss over
positive sin with those hypocritical palliations
which the most hardened are constrained to
offer as a salve to their conscience. She knew
other women—too many of them—some indeed whom society had established at its head
— who were far more guilty in deed to their
husbands than she had ever been. But the
consciousness of others' impurity was no excuse
for that infidelity of thought of which she was

alone guilty, but which, in her own eyes, was a deadly sin.   It is hard to blame her for those human emotions which, seek to control them as we may, will have their way.   I think some mercy, even from the most severe in such matters, is to be shown to the woman who tramples her feelings under her feet, if she cannot crush them in her heart, that she may walk steadily in that path of duty every step of which costs a bitter pain.

She was interrupted in her reveries by the entrance of her cousin.

'Well, *ma belle comtesse*,' he said, good-humouredly ; 'superbly beautiful as ever, I see.   Marriage, according to all accounts, has much to answer for in many cases ; but, at any rate, it cannot be reproached with having rendered you less charming.'

'Pray don't flatter in that open fashion,' she answered, pettishly.   'It reminds me of the days when I was weak and vain enough to be gratified with such utter worthlessness.'

'My dear Edith,' he said, gravely, 'don't snub me in that heartless manner.   I have a dim suspicion I lost you through lack of

paying proper compliments, and I was trying
to supply the deficiencies of my neglected
education in this respect.'

'Compliments would not win me if I were
free once more,' she said.

'You say so,' he returned, lightly, 'because
there is so little chance of your being free
again. Lord Ardross is one of those hale,
hearty individuals of whom one could safely
predict he would live beyond all reasonable
expectations and wishes—a veritable matrimonial "old man of the mountain," who will
shake his wife off instead of letting her get
rid of him.'

'I have no wish to shake him off, as you
call it,' she exclaimed, passionately; 'and his
is the last name that *your* lips should couple
with a heartless jest. You have done him
injury enough already. At least have the
decency to refrain from vilifying him to the
ears of his wife.'

Carnmore looked at her rather surprised for
a moment; then, recovering himself quickly,
he answered, with a cool shrug of his
shoulders—

'I humbly apologise for putting you in a passion, my fair cousin. It was mere thoughtlessness that led me to introduce Lord Ardross's name into my conversation. Henceforth I will take care not to offend in a similar manner. May he live to the age of Methuselah, if he finds such longevity comfortable.'

'Always a sneer,' she said, bitterly. 'That mocking tongue has been, and will always be, your curse through life. Do you know,' she added presently, regarding him fixedly, 'much as you affect to despise my husband because he is not what the world calls intellectual— because he cannot satirise his friends and lash his enemies with the skill you do—his is the nobler nature of the two? I like him well enough to know that.'

'You are scarcely complimentary, Edith,' he answered coolly. He was not easily to be offended that day. 'You consured my want of decency just now: have you ever thought I am the last person to whom you should recite your husband's perfection, especially when I am such a sufferer in your eyes by the contrast?'

'I beg your pardon,' she replied. 'I did not see it in that light at the moment, but I understand it now, Fred. You have no cause to be friends to each other, of course.'

'And peace is restored between us,' he said, good-humouredly. 'Well, it is better than quarrelling. We have done with all that folly, I hope. It did not particularly promote our happiness when we practised it.'

The coolness of his tone somewhat galled her. Although it was herself that had forbidden him to speak openly of their past love, yet, in his covert allusions he always contrived to introduce a sneer that grated painfully on her proud and sensitive nature.

They sat silent for some moments, Carnmore watching, with a strange blending of emotion, the fair face on which their recent passage-at-arms had raised a look of vexation and mortification, till he said, 'I had the pleasure of making a new acquaintance last night, Edith. Someone you must know too.'

'A woman?' she asked. 'I suppose it's a woman, or you wouldn't take such interest in telling me.' A little bit of pique would show itself.

'Your conjecture is most sagacious,' he said. He had noticed the pique in her tone, and rather derived gratification from the fact. 'It was a woman, and whom do you imagine? None other than your successor to the chair of Beauty, left vacant by your marriage, Miss Maud Hilton.'

'And what do you think of her?' asked Edith, curtly.

'I have met her a few times before; but it was only last night that I had an opportunity of gauging her powers and claims to distinction, and the conclusion I have arrived at is that the encomiums lavished on her beauty are justly merited, and that she possesses talents and character far above the common.'

'You are *épris*, then, I suppose,' was Edith's rejoinder.

Carnmore laughed easily. 'I am not Miss Hilton's slave as yet,' he said. 'I don't betray any symptoms of the love-malady to-day, do I?'

'You are not an easy book to read,' she

answered, coldly. 'There are crabbed and crooked characters in your pages difficult to decipher.'

'Like yourself, then, fair countess,' he replied, gaily ; 'but in this instance I am as legible as print. I am not *épris* with Miss Hilton ; I only admire her.'

'And admiration not unfrequently ends in love.'

'True,' he said, thoughtfully, and watching the effect of his words upon her, 'I might end, as you say, by loving Maud. I suppose such a thing is not absolutely impossible ; a man's heart must be capacious enough to hold a second image beside the first.'

'Man's heart,' answered Edith, with haughty scorn, 'is a vast receptacle for all kinds of worthless emotions. It can accommodate a hundred idols at once, and be hypocrite enough to pretend it worships them all.'

'You are severe upon us,' retorted Carnmore, with a smile. 'We are not baser deceivers than many among your sex.'

'Perhaps not,' she answered, impatiently. 'The worse for our sex, then.'

'You see, my dear Edith,' he said, in that calm, *reasoning* tone, that he knew was especially aggravating to the woman beside him, 'marriage is an honourable and exceedingly fashionable institution. When a man is only an honourable, or a probable heir to great expectations, he can do very well without it; but when the coronet of his father presses upon his brow, and he is expected to perpetuate the family honours, it then becomes a serious question. A man can't exist upon a pure Platonic attachment, however pleasant it may be—can he?'

'I suppose not,' she answered, coldly and curtly.

'We don't find the ladies capable of such a sacrifice,' he continued, 'although theirs is the sex to whom we usually look for examples of disinterestedness. So we are hardly to blame if we fail in what even they cannot achieve.'

'No one is blaming you that I am aware of,' she answered.

'I know that,' he answered, gravely; 'but supposing—I say supposing, for as yet I have not the remotest intention of trying to carry my words into effect—that I married Maud Hilton, should I be free from blame in your eyes then?'

She paused for an instant; then she spoke haughtily and distinctly:

'Lord Carnmore, the compact between us is that of friendship. However we may have loved once, the past is buried now, and I have no claim upon you that should make me the arbiter of your destiny. When you choose a wife, dispense with the mockery of asking my consent. It is as hypocritical in you as it is distasteful to me.'

'I thank you for your candour,' he said, slowly and bitterly. 'I have rigidly observed the conditions on which you permitted our acquaintance. This is the first time that I have ventured to infringe them; and, considering the past, of which you choose to speak so scornfully, I should have imagined I might have expected, I will not say kinder, for that is incompatible with your nature, but more *womanly*, treatment at your hands.'

'I am sorry to have disappointed you,' she

answered, coldly. 'You will probably receive both from Miss Hilton.'

'I can believe one thing, at least, of her,' he said, angrily : 'she would not sacrifice human hearts to her vanity, only to make a jest of their sufferings after.' And, with that bitter speech, he left.

They were both wroth with each other : she, because she resented even the hint of infidelity implied in his union with another ; he, because he considered that, knowing the circumstances of his deep and unsatisfied love, she might have spoken or acted in a way that should have shown she took such an interest in him that she could not bear the thought of his belonging to anyone else ;—a mutual mis-understanding, such as that which had wrecked their happiness in the old days, and which, persisted in now, should bring even more bitter remorse to themselves and others than any that had come before. And Edith buried her haughty head upon the table beside her, and wept those fierce, scalding tears of peni-tence and passion which, God forbid, it is the hard lot of many creatures on this earth to shed.

Verily, there is need of a wise and mighty Judge to temper the wind to the shorn lamb. Well is it for many of us that there be hope of peace in another world; for, otherwise, our hearts would break in the trouble and turmoil of this.

CHAPTER IX.

'COMPARISON.'

'I WILL wager a cool hundred Ollinski has received his *congé*. There's an air of sulky dignity about a man who has been rejected that's not to be mistaken.'

So spoke that veteran man of the world, the Honourable Harry Desmond, to his young friend and social pupil, Lord Windermere. He was initiating the inexperienced viscount into the mysteries of life—*i.e.*, fast life; and took care to pay himself pretty well out of the process. Mr. Desmond was a by no means uncommon type of the impecunious class of younger sons who are, comparatively speaking, thrown on their own resources for the means of mixing with their more fortunate brethren. It is delightful to note how Providence has marked its sense of the disparity between rich and poor by usually giving the latter a much superior cerebral development. I think Mr. Desmond could scarcely have afforded the Chancellor of the Exchequer a very lucid explanation of the various sources from whence he derived a tolerably comfortable income. He speculated slightly on the Stock Exchange, and was unrivalled in the cunning lore of backing horses till winning was reduced to a positive certainty. He also excelled in all games of skill and chance, and few older men could 'pluck a pigeon' more cleanly or skilfully. Not a very nice character, perhaps. But we can scarcely blame him, or others like him : such men are the production of our imperfect social morality.

In the conjecture which he hazarded to the inexperienced ears of his friend Lord Windermere Mr. Desmond was perfectly correct. Maud Hilton had rejected the man whom, at one time, she had almost learned to regard as her future husband. How strange are the caprices of the human heart ! She could have married Ollinski, although she knew he could never have moved her heart deeply. Saville she liked as a friend more than anyone; yet to him she could not have sacrificed her life, had all the social advantages of the prince been his.

She could not deny to herself that the sound of Carnmore's voice, the most indifferent glance from him, awoke in her a sweet and powerful emotion, which she could not understand if it were not akin to love. Such women as Maud Hilton rarely experience any of those youthful sensations which inexperience takes for deep and abiding passion. When their heart once wakes from its lethargy, it awakes with a convulsive bound, to pour forth the full and unchecked tide of virginal emotion. There must have been a strange fascination in Carnmore to arouse the same powerful love in two such opposite temperaments as those of Maud and Edith.

And was his heart touched or not by the beauty he had admired with the eye, by the nature he had found so pure? Truly, I think so. There is a love born of passion, and a love born of admiration. Edith and Maud were so totally different, they could never have aroused the same passion. The one fiery, impulsive, impassioned; the other calm, equable, and deep; and, yet, in both the sweet genuine warmth of woman nature. It was the difference between the scorching heavens of the desert, and the soft, sunny skies of the south. Yet I do not mean to infer by this that Maud Hilton could not love with all the same intensity as Edith. I believe, on the contrary, that hers would have been the *safer* love of the two. She would have forgiven more, made more excuses for her lover than the other. A little would have turned Edith's passionate love into as passionate hate; but I think Maud Hilton's heart, once won, could never have utterly banished all tenderness from it, even though it had been wounded to the death.

Yes, in those days Maud had an empire over his heart. I do not mean to say that the glamour of the first love was shed over the second. Man, or woman either, can only love intensely once in their lives: it may be in their youth, or in their prime; but, whenever

it comes, that one deep love is writ in glowing
characters that will never fade, that may be
imitated in an after-time, but never reproduced.
Still he loved her with a love that was pure
and true. And he admired her, perhaps, even
more than he loved her : for sometimes noble
qualities compel an involuntary worship that
is in itself a love for their possessor.

Nor is it unlikely that Edith's recent coldness had rendered him more than ever
susceptible to another influence. He could
scarcely guess the cause of that estrangement
which was gradually creeping between them.
Few women are just where they love. She
would have kept him by her side for ever,
heedless of the sacrifice she exacted from
him—a sacrifice to which, too, she could give
none in return. She had proved herself
faithless in deed to him, but it was galling to
her that he should requite it with a similar
infidelity. Moreover, there was another thing
that disquieted her sorely—as it ever will in
such cases—she could read her own feelings,
but she could only guess at his. Even in that
very marriage in which, as it were, her false-

ness was indelibly commemorated, she knew herself that she had really given him no rival in her heart. Much as she liked her husband, what was he to her life in comparison with the other? The earth is lighted by the sun and moon, but in which does it love to bask the most—in the pure, calm radiance of the one, or in the warm, lurid beams that the brighter luminary flings over its brother planet? How could she be sure of man's constancy? Bright eyes and sweet lips!—do not men thirst to gaze in the one, to lay kisses on the other? Can *one* hope to slake for ever that mad lust of beauty? Fidelity is a strange thing. There are some who keep faithful from having too little emotion, some from having too much; but I think the best and purest among men are far behind women in that greatest virtue of love.

The Derby had come and gone: the usual number of people ruined in consequence, the usual amount of suicides, the ordinary amount of defalcations of speculative clerks, had attested the beneficial effects of this turf saturnalia. Ascot was not far off, and the

London season altogether was in its meridian. Still, Maud Hilton's name was not coupled officially with that of any male 'eligibility.' Public opinion rather inclined to Carnmore as the probable 'conquering hero,' but wise people remembered the devotedness of Prince Ollinski, and shook their heads when anything serious was hinted.

They had abundant opportunities of meeting, of course. Very often they were guests together at Lord Ravensworth's. This nobleman had been an intimate friend of the late Lord Carnmore. Although descended from a family of great antiquity, by the side of which those who boasted that they 'came over with the Conqueror' seemed but as men of yesterday, he was a man of liberal and enlightened views. It was only natural that his friendship for the father should dispose him favourably towards the son; and, in addition to this reason for cultivating his acquaintance, Carnmore was already a prominent man in the House of Lords and among his party; one, therefore, to whom it behoved a veteran politician like

Lord Ravensworth to show respect and con
sideration.

They met one night, a few days before
Ascot, at dinner at his house.   Maud had
been delivered to the care of an ambassador
of great diplomatic renown, and Carnmore
had been fain to content himself with taking
charge of a rather fast, yet withal fascinating,
young lady, who had been invested by her
mother with a roving commission to catch a
husband in the best way she could.   To such a
prudent and worldly-minded young personage
twenty-five thousand a year and a coronet were
a consideration ; and she was not long before
she directed her powers against Carnmore.
That gentleman knew quite enough of the
young lady's character to fathom her motives,
and, though somewhat disgusted, contrived to
flirt with her sufficiently to excite no small
hopes in her ambitious bosom.   On entering
the drawing-room afterwards, the young
maiden was unfortunately doomed to bitter
disappointment, for he crossed over immediately to Maud.

She welcomed him with a slight smile, and

a rather more palpable colour on her fair cheek; and the Earl of Morton, who had been doing his best to entertain her hitherto, moved away at the advent of the new comer.

'I have been sadly victimised at dinner,' he said, with a smile. 'Did you observe who was my companion?'

'Florence Egerton,' she answered, with just a shade of contempt in her voice. 'One of those young ladies who are professional husband-hunters, and will sell themselves to the highest bidder.'

'You seem very indignant over it,' said Carnmore.

'I am,' she replied, earnestly. 'When I see such girls as that trampling all their woman's best and purest feelings beneath their feet, I despise my own sex, or, rather, I should say, the travestie of it.'

'Aye,' said Carnmore, thoughtfully, 'it is, as you say, thoroughly contemptible; yet, what a few women we find not inoculated with the sordid taint! That you have contrived to escape it is not a wonder, for your

nature would scarce permit you to do otherwise; but it is, at least, to your credit that
you keep yourself healthy amongst permanent
disease.'

'I thank heaven that in that respect, at
any rate, I have not to blush for myself. My
love may be won, but the riches of the world
could not purchase it.'

'And, yet, I have sometimes heard you
regret you were a woman.'

'What has that wish to do with what I have
just said?'

'Because,' he answered, slowly, 'love that
may be wooed, but cannot be bought, is an
infinitely greater blessing, in my opinion, to a
woman than a man. I believe that the purest
and noblest love is felt only by your sex. We
love passionately and deeply, it is true, but
our passion is selfish. We can make sacrifices,
but we must exact sacrifices in return; we
demand fidelity in thought and deed, but how
seldom can we proffer it in exchange. And,
therefore, I say, that the love which gives all,
yet exacts little—that pardons until "seventy
times seven"—that is pure, steady, and un-

wavering—such is the love of woman, and not of man, and happy and blessed is that woman in whom it can be awakened.'

'Is the capacity to love such a blessing, after all?' she asked, dubiously. 'Some people say not.'

'Cold, worldly-wise cynics,' he answered, 'who, because they are emotionless themselves, exalt it into a virtue. It may be that those whose feelings are intense reap sorrow even greater than their joy; but I contend that five minutes' happiness of those to whom nature has given the capacity of emotion is worth the lifetime that the others drag on, secure in their selfish indifference to aught that is beautiful or exquisite. The heart without love is like a diamond without the light, like a flower without the sun.'

'You are right, I think,' she answered, thoughtfully. 'As you say, those who feel must know bitter sorrow as well as exquisite joy. Yet, who would not brave the dangers and the coldness of the deep for the priceless pearls that lay strewn beneath its waves? Yes, I would sooner love, were it to my own destruction, than leave life with my heart mute in a long eternal sleep.'

The light of love trembled in her eyes as she spoke, his ensign deepened on her cheek, his eloquence animated her lips. A few short weeks ago she could only have dreamt of his power; now she had known it.

'Do not sigh because you are a woman, Miss Hilton,' he said, earnestly. 'Do not envy us our energy, our strength, our ambition. You have the greater empire over the two: we can command all things, but you command us.'

'How can we have empire over you?' she answered, almost bitterly, 'when our love makes us your slaves.'

'Nay,' he said, in a low voice, 'it is we who wear the chain; it is your hand that imposes it on us.' There was a ring of passion in his tones as he uttered those words that told his own heart was not quite indifferent; and, in that mood, it is impossible to say what he might not have added, if Mrs. Jerningham had not at that moment approached them.

'You are appropriating Maud dreadfully this evening,' she said, gaily, to Carnmore, 'and I am dying to have a gossip with her. We have not met for a week, and must have a whole budget of news to communicate to each other.'

'I will take the hint and retire,' said Carnmore, good-humouredly. 'As Sir Peter Teazle says, "I leave my character in your hands."'

He sat a long time over his cigar that night, puffing at it very slowly, as he pondered over the events of the day. He felt Maud Hilton was becoming dearer to him than he had ever thought was possible of another woman. Was it improbable that it should end in marriage? Presently he rose and took a portrait of Edith out of his desk. He gazed on it long and earnestly, and then laid it down with a deep sigh.

'Strange!' he murmured to himself: 'the one woman shocks my fastidiousness in a thousand things ; the other comes up to my notion of an almost perfect ideal. I have proved Edith's falsehood ; I know Maud could never be aught but pure and true. Yet, if the two stood before me at this moment, both free, what is this accursed spell upon me that would make me choose the worst?'

CHAPTER X.

'AN UNFATHOMABLE SORROW.'

LORD RAVENSWORTH owned a somewhat small, but elegantly built, villa on the banks of the Thames, a little above Richmond. He made frequent use of this residence, both for himself and his friends, in the season. The cool glades and the tranquil water were both refreshing to a man often fatigued with his senatorial duties. He had great taste, and his toy villa, simple and unpretending as it looked, was the repository of some great curiosities in art. He belonged to that old school, so rapidly dying out amongst us, who judge for themselves in nearly everything they have to purchase. The present generation leaves the choice of its furniture to the upholsterer, and

the arrangement of its dinners to its cook.
We buy second-rate wines, for which we pay
first-rate prices, and bid for pictures because
it is the fashion to ornament our rooms, not
because we have any real liking for art.   Our
forefathers had a good many vices that have
since become unfashionable, and no inconsiderable amount of virtues that are equally
despised nowadays ; but I think they contrived to get better money's worth for their
money than their descendants are in the habit
of doing, in spite of the increased 'cuteness on
which they pride themselves.

His lordship had invited a few select guests
as permanent visitors.   The dimensions of
his villa would not permit of many, and he
supplemented these by reinforcements of
London pilgrims to dinners and dances.
Carnmore was included among the former :
first, because he was a man whose literary
and social position demanded consideration ;
and, secondly, because the party to which
they both belonged was at that period meditating a flank movement on the government,
and the consultations between the political

generals and lieutenants were necessarily frequent and mysterious. The atmosphere of intrigue was one which suited Lord Ravensworth's constitution well. He was somewhat old-fashioned in his notions of conducting legislation. He resembled the reticent politician of old times, before the inundation of newspapers and a more general frankness of speech and tone consequent upon social improvement had penetrated the veil of mystery that had hitherto usually enshrouded their proceedings.

Maud Hilton was there too, with her father and mother. Mr. Hilton was a handsome florid man, in whom a certain rustic heartiness contended with the *nonchalance* of fashionable training. He represented his county in the House; but, beyond unflinching allegiance to the 'whip,' and a periodical address to his constituents, in which he would dwell with considerable unction on the 'great legislative results of the session,' his parliamentary career was not remarkable. He was a safe man on committees, and had a reputation for good dinners; but within the walls of St. Stephen's he was, like little children are told they should be, 'seen, not heard.'

Mrs. Hilton was a fine type of matronly beauty. The wear and tear of London life had spared her pretty well. Her figure, like those of a great many other women of her age, was addicted to what Hawthorne described as 'beefiness,' but it was shapely withal; and her clear cut features were scarcely less beautiful than in the days when the Honourable Maud L'Estrange created almost as much sensation in society as her daughter had done at the present time. Mrs. Hilton was a clever woman of the world, with no small natural abilities; but I don't think Maud had derived her earnest nature either from her father or mother.

Carnmore met Saville accidentally the day before he was going down to Richmond. The latter had only returned lately from a somewhat prolonged visit to a friend in the north, and was crossing St. James's Park on his way from a morning sitting in the House. Carnmore turned back to walk with him.

'My dear fellow,' he said, cordially, 'I

thought I was never going to see you again,
you have become such a hermit. What has
society been particularly guilty in lately that
you avoid it so ? '

Saville smiled slightly at his friend's banter-
ing tone.

' I have no especially fresh quarrel with the
world,' he said, ' only I am getting older,
and, I suppose, more impatient in consequence.
The husband cannot endure the petulance in
a wife that he had tolerated in the mistress,
and, probably, it is the same with me. What
youth regarded as folly, middle age condemns
as sin.'

' You seem to be growing very misanthro-
pical,' answered Carnmore. ' It is no use
shutting yourself up and railing at mankind.
At any rate, if you despise your own sex so,
begin a fresh experience with the other. The
women have a little heart left still, in spite of
the general decay of virtue.'

Saville made some short and jesting answer
to this, and they walked on in silence for some
seconds, till Carnmore spoke again.

' I am going down to Richmond to-morrow

to stay for a few days with Ravensworth. It
will be an agreeable change from the hot
metropolis.'

'And Ravensworth will make a pleasant
host : he possesses the courtesy of the old-
fashioned school. It would be as well if his
politics were not quite so old-fashioned,
too.'

'Ah !' answered Carnmore, with a smile,
' he is not the stuff of which Radicals are made.
He will do all he can to make his inferior
brethren happy and contented, but he must
shower his benefits from a pedestal; he
cannot stand on the same ground with them.
By the way,' he added, presently, ' I have
not been able to tell you some news I wanted
on account of your absence. I have met your
friend, Miss Hilton, and we have become
great allies. She tells me that you and she
were very intimate before you turned into
such a hermit.'

'Yes, we used to get on very well together,'
he answered, calmly. His friend little knew
what an effort that calmness cost him. 'She
was so thoroughly free from the frivolity and

littleness of ordinary women, that she suited
my somewhat fastidious taste.'

'And yet you did not fall in love with her?'
asked Carnmore, curiously.

'My dear fellow, does love necessarily
follow admiration?'

'Necessarily? No. Very often? Yes. All
admiration does not end in love, but all love
begins with admiration.'

'You are exceedingly logical to-day,' said
Saville, laughing. 'But you have had great
experience in love, so I suppose I must allow
you to be a judge.'

They walked on till they arrived at Saville's
lodgings. 'You will come in and have some
lunch,' he said, as his friend held out his
hand at the door.

'Thanks, no,' answered Carnmore : 'I have
some calls to make, and am not overburdened
with time. I will come and see you as soon
as I return from Richmond. You must turn
over a new leaf then, and come and abuse
society to its face a bit. I can't quite make
out what it is, but there seems to have come
an extraordinary change over you lately.'

'Idle fancies,' returned Saville, lightly: 'I am the same as ever—I despise mankind, and loathe injustice; I compassionate the weak, I lift my voice against the strong, who grind them under their heel; and I shall do so till the day of my death. If you have anything to do with my tombstone, inscribe those virtues on it.'

'May that day be far off,' cried Carnmore, gaily. '*Au revoir.*' And he turned away.

Yes, he was right, a change had come over Saville. Man of the world, philosopher as he was, that deep love had defied oblivion, had revealed the impotence of philosophy to subdue nature. It had come to him later than it comes to most, and he had atoned for his years of temperance by such deep intoxication that it had made him a slave, the chains of whose bondage must be worn till death.

CHAPTER XI.

'A BAPTISM OF TEARS.'

THE last visit Carnmore paid before starting
for Lord Ravensworth's was to Edith. There
had been a certain coldness between them ever
since the day when he had first mentioned
Maud's name to her, and their greeting to-day
was somewhat constrained. Even as friends
they could not be sweet-tempered for long.

They talked on indifferent subjects for a
little while, and then Carnmore let her know
that it was in some measure a farewell visit.

'I am going down to Richmond to-day to
spend a week or two with Ravensworth. You
know him, of course?'

'Miss Hilton's uncle,' I think, she answered,
calmly.

'Miss Hilton's uncle,' he repeated, in a
slightly embarrassed tone. 'He and I are

great political allies, and we intend mapping out a grand campaign against the government while I am down there.'

Edith's lip curled ever so slightly. 'I wish you success in your wonderful schemes,' she said, with a suspicion of sarcasm in her voice; 'and, further, that you may enjoy to the full the agreeable society you will meet at his house.'

'Come, Edith,' answered her cousin, with a rather amused expression on his face, 'you are really getting too polite. You are uttering a string of little commonplace platitudes on everything I tell you, as if I were the most ordinary acquaintance in the world.'

Edith shrugged her shoulders with a depreciating air. 'I never did succeed in pleasing you in anything I said or did yet. I suppose it is too late in the day to hope for your approbation now?'

'I will certainly compliment you on one thing, my fair cousin,' he answered, gravely— 'an accomplishment you possess to perfection; and that is the art of making a quarrel out of nothing.'

' Thank you,' she said, calmly. ' You were always a bad hand at compliments, at least to me. I have no doubt that, to other people, you are amiability itself.'

' Now, Edith, my dear child,' he said, pleadingly, ' don't let us run colloquial tilts against each other. We are both probably good hands at saying cutting and unpleasant things ; but suppose we exercise our talents on somebody else, not on ourselves? Besides, I really want to tell you something rather serious.'

' Deliver yourself of your important matter, pray,' she answered, leaning back in her chair very composedly.

Carnmore hesitated for a moment. The subject on which he proposed to enter was a somewhat embarrassing one, but at last he plucked up heart of grace, and said, in a rather low voice—' The fact of it is, I have nearly made up my mind to propose to Maud Hilton.'

Not a muscle of her face moved as he said this, although her heart seemed almost to cease throbbing for an instant. Her face was perhaps a shade paler than its wont as she answered—

'And that, I presume, is the object that takes you down to Richmond ? '

'Yes,' he answered, with a sigh of what seemed relief to think that the announcement was received so comfortably and calmly. He knew that at one time Edith's pride was such that she would have sooner cut out her tongue than remonstrate with her lover's infidelity, but she had changed greatly since then, and he had not been altogether certain as to the manner in which she would take it.

'I suppose I can only offer my sincerest congratulations ?' she said, presently.

'You are too polite,' he said, impatiently. 'I had not the hypocrisy to congratulate you on your marriage. You might at least imitate my sincerity. Besides, you are rather premature ; the young lady has not accepted me as yet.'

'I don't expect there will be much doubt of that,' she replied, sneeringly. 'Miss Hilton has, no doubt, been brought up well, and she will look at twenty-five thousand a year and a coronet from a proper point of view.'

Carnmore frowned slightly. 'You mistake her character altogether,' he said, sternly. 'Whether she accepted me or not, I would stake my life on her truth and purity. It is precisely because she is so superior to ordinary women, and so removed from worldly littleness, that I have thought of her as a wife.'

'I beg your pardon,' answered Edith, coldly: 'I have no doubt Miss Hilton is the perfect paragon you believe her.'

'I don't believe in paragons at all, as it happens,' he said, angrily; 'but I think she is a woman whom a man may take in perfect safety for his wife, and not be tormented every hour with the fear that her frivolous conduct may break his heart, if it does not bring upon him positive shame.'

'I can only repeat, success to your wooing.'

'I don't suppose I am a very honourable lover,' he said, bitterly, 'to offer a pure and virtuous girl the mere remnants of a heart, and lead her to believe she is the dearest to me on earth.'

'There need be little apprehension on that score,' answered Edith, scornfully. 'No man can be so insensate as to remain long obdurate to the influence of such virtues as you ascribe to her.'

'Unfortunately, it is not always the deserving who reap the love they should,' he said, ironically. 'Hearts seem generally playing at cross purposes in this world. Men, as a rule, waste their love on worthless women, who are too heartless to even comprehend the feelings they excite; and the few women who love waste it, nine times out of ten, on a barren and sterile soil, or, worse still, on men who can appreciate, but have not the power to requite 't.'

'True,' she answered, bitterly; 'but I will tell you one thing as equally certain. Men and women can both love intensely, but there is this great difference between them—a woman may be faithless in deed, but never in thought; a man can be false in both.'

'The thought matters little if the deed gives the lie to it,' he said, sternly, as he rose from his chair.

She rose too, and held out her hand. He took it, and took hold of her left as well, and stood there with her two hands held firmly in his own, looking gravely in her face, with mute lips and passion-speaking eyes. None the less had the fiery breath of passion scorched her heart. Those dark, brilliant eyes were as eloquent with the language of love as those which looked into them. There they stood, she the wife of another, he the wooer of another; both false, unutterably false in deed, but as true to each other in heart and soul as though an indissoluble union had linked their fates together for henceforth and for ever.

There was such deep, unfathomable love in those mournful-speaking eyes that sought her own, that something like a tear trembled on her cheek as she turned her face away.

'Edith,' he said, sadly, drawing her closely to him, 'your tears and my prayers are powerless to recall the past; but, God be my witness, I would sooner have never been born than live as I do now, to curse the love I bear you.'

She lifted up to him the tear-stained face,

from which all the petulance and pride were vanished, and laid her lips to his in a mute, passionate caress.

'Forgive me, my darling, if you can,' she whispered; 'and may God grant you may be happier with another than you would have ever been with me.'

He smiled a sad, weary, heart-broken smile. 'Never so happy with another as with you,' he said, mournfully. 'I would wait now were there hope; but it is only death that can unbind your chains. It was your own hand that wrought our misery; we must bear it all our days. You will not repair the wrong you have done. You may be right; but that determination shuts out from us all hopes of happiness for ever.'

And so they parted in a rather sad fashion, his wooing with another baptised with her tears.

.He drove down to Richmond, a prey to mingled feelings. He loved Maud dearly he knew, but the shadow of that great passion of his life was on his heart, and it seemed as if he were going to raise a barrier between himself and that first love greater than any that had loomed before.

Far different were the feelings with which Maud awaited his advent. Her whole heart was given to him—no shadow of the past obtruded its sombre gloom upon her young life. She guessed, with a woman's instinct, that he loved her; and as she sat in her chamber dreaming that sweet dream which we have all of us had once in our lives, and wondering whether their union would ever be, she descried his carriage driving along the avenue, and all at once her eyes were sparkling, and her cheeks were crimsoning, with the tender light of love.

CHAPTER XII.

'THE WOOING 'O'T.'

How agreeable they are, those small parties, composed exclusively of clever and companion-able people. Lord Ravensworth was always especially happy in his selection of guests. He regarded them in much the same light as a cook regards his materials—as so many different compounds to be mixed together in one homogeneous whole. Carnmore had seldom enjoyed any visit so much as those few days he passed at Richmond.

There were no professional female or male flirts among the party; so he was not in dread of a rival for Maud Hilton's favour. Lord Ravensworth's guests were in society, but they belonged to the intellectual portion of it—that portion which is obliged sometimes to mix among the mere devotees of fashion and *ton*, but generally contrives to hold itself aloof from them.

Neither Mr. nor Mrs. Hilton, who I forgot to state had been a novelist of some note in her younger days, were unconscious of the attentions which Carnmore now plainly showed to their daughter; but they were both too wise to attempt to force her inclinations either way. Mrs. Hilton was worldly clever, but Maud was intellectually clever, and the former lady stood somewhat in awe of sustaining an argument with her daughter. On the one occasion that she had attempted to influence her with regard to Prince Ollinski, Maud had answered quietly, but firmly—

'Mamma, I shall never marry any man I do not love. Some girls may think it proper to marry for position, and to please their worldly relatives, but such sordid principles are not mine. I shall never love unworthily, I know; but I would marry the man who won my heart, perfectly indifferent as to whether he had five hundred or five millions.'

However much Mrs. Hilton might have

advocated love matches in her novels, as
finding them more popular in consequence, it
is doubtful whether she fully recognised their
expediency in real life.   At any rate, she did
not attempt to openly coerce her daughter's
sentiments, but contented herself with re-
marking to her husband that Maud was a
strange, romantic girl.   It may easily be
guessed that a man of Carnmore's celebrity,
both in literature and politics, would not prove
an unacceptable son-in-law in her eyes, even
had not his title and fortune already furnished
sufficient recommendations.

He had been four days down at Richmond
already, and still he rather hung back from
the task he had imposed on himself, although
he felt that every hour he spent with Maud
increased his admiration for her.   But it is
not an easy thing for a man oscillating between
two loves to decide on a step that shall shut
him out completely from the other.   While
he had his freedom he could always take
advantage of any opportunity that arose with
regard to Edith.   Her husband might die ; it
was extremely improbable, of course, but not

impossible : healthy and strong men have
been known to go off without the least expectation on the part of their relatives. Even
her own resolution might wax fainter in time.
There are so many chances for the lover of a
married woman—temporary unkindnesses on
the part of the husband, suspicion on the part
of society which almost hints the sin to which
she is urged—it must be a determined woman
who can wage successful war against her own
heart for alway, when the voice of the tempter
is ever sounding in her ears.

All this he thought of in those four days in
which he meditated so constantly to himself.
If he pledged himself to Maud, he was binding
around him chains from which he could never
escape, save with a double dishonour. In
spite of that passion for Edith, he had sufficient conscience left for another. He had
gauged Maud's nature thoroughly : he knew
she would be purity and devotion itself to the
man she loved ; and he loathed the idea of ever
requiting her constancy by infidelity with
another. If he married her, he was bound to
look upon Edith as dead to him, as completely

removed from him as if she had been lying in her grave, far beyond the reach of hopeless passion.

Besides, his loyalty to Edith was still strong. That strange and fantastic morality to which he subjected their loves compelled him to regard himself as bound to her still, in spite of that infidelity which should have released him from all other obligation.   As it was with the guilty love of Lancelot, so he felt—

His honour, rooted in dishonour, stood ;
And faith, unfaithful, kept him falsely true.

It was a hard struggle, this contest between a love that had armed reason on its side, and a mad, restless passion that reason could not excuse ; but, at length, he allowed the former to conquer, and he determined to take the first opportunity of asking Maud to be his wife.   He had little doubt in his own mind as to the success of his wooing.   He was learned in love by now, and he had read something of her heart—sufficient to make him think she cared for him.

Opportunity was not long in presenting itself.   In the evening the guests betook them-

selves to various amusements.   Some were
in the billiard-room, others at cards ; some in
the drawing-room, solacing themselves with
music.   The windows of this apartment opened
on a terrace, from which steps, at regular
intervals, led on to the lawn.   It was one of
those calm, almost breathless, summer evenings
which are so enjoyable in the country, and a
few of the visitors had taken advantage of the
beautiful night to stroll about the grounds.

Carnmore and Maud both preferred the
calm summer air to the heated atmosphere of
the saloon, and wandered about for some time
together, both indifferent as to the possible
impropriety of the proceeding.   As Carnmore
had once said, on a similar occasion, they both
possessed reputations above the scandal of
drawing-rooms.

They both stopped at last close to the river,
which looked very tranquil, sleeping under the
soft, clear rays of the moon, and the twinkling
lights of a thousand stars shimmering on its
bosom.

'What a glorious night!' exclaimed Maud,
as her eyes drank in the tender beauty of that

moonlit scene. 'Is it not one especially meant for poets?'

Her companion's voice sounded very rich and earnest as he answered—

'Rather is it not one meant for lovers?'

A slight flush suffused the clear marble of her cheek as she said—

'Perhaps so. What a double inspiration, then, for one who combines the poet with the lover!'

'Were I a woman,' he said, gravely, 'it is such a one who should win me, and I would be wooed at an hour and in a spot like this. Love is beautiful in itself, and all around it should reflect its beauty.'

There was a sweet tenderness in his voice that made her feel strangely happy. The clearness of the skies above, the tranquil mirroring waters, rendered sombre here and there by the quivering shadows of the trees, which murmured a gentle wordless music as the soft night wind stole through their leaves, were in harmony with her heart. It was, in truth, a fitting scene for love.

'How beautiful,' he said, presently, 'if

love could always live in the paradise it first paints for itself; if the coarse voices, the sordid cares and ambitions of the world, could never disturb its repose !'

' It is possible that they never should,' she answered, earnestly. 'Love can live in the world, and yet trust to its own purity and intensity to lift it to something higher. The eagle builds his nest in the rock, but he has the heavens for his empire.'

' Aye,' he answered, tenderly, 'with you, perhaps, such a paradise might be, for you are as different from woman as the eagle is superior to his kind.'

The flickering flushes came and went on her cheek, as she heard that unmistakable language of love. He drew her closely towards him, and his lips almost touched hers as he whispered—

' Could a poet err in gauging a nature so like his own ? On the first night we met I read in your eyes candour and purity. I gathered from your words scorn for the sordid, hatred for the false. I loved you so much because I felt what you felt, because I honoured what you honoured, and despised what you despised. Tell me, Maud, can our lives be twain, even as our natures are ?'

He bent over her fondly, and, reading his answer in her eyes, sealed his love upon her lips.

'You love me, my darling?' he asked, tenderly.

'More than life or aught beside,' was the earnest answer; and her radiant beauty seemed to take new life and light as she spoke, for love had breathed into it a soul.

CHAPTER XIII.

'NOT UTTERLY BANISHED.'

VERY sweet were those early love days with
Maud. There was no petulance, no inconsiderate anger; none of those abrupt transitions
from one mood to another, which had so
disturbed the first wooing. It was a silken
chain he wore now, but its wearing never
fretted nor galled. The innate honour that
was Maud's dominant characteristic governed
her actions in every relation of life. It was
her creed that she owed nearly as much fealty
to an acknowledged lover as to a husband.
If she disliked flirtation when she was free, a
thousand times more did she despise it now
that she was bound to another. She had an
equal contempt for those petty arts which
women do not scruple to make use of in order

to display their power over their lover. Neither was she unreasonably jealous: she was too pure herself to suspect impurity in others. Things which would have driven Edith to distraction scarcely disturbed her tranquil bosom, although she would have been inflexible and unpardoning to an open infidelity.

Neither did she attempt to conceal her love. She was not ashamed to let him know that he was the dearest on earth to her. The paltry pride which exacts affection and refuses to exhibit it in return was beneath her. Had she parted from him to-morrow, she would never have denied the depth of her love for him. Very sweet and tender, too, were some of those confessions which lovers do their best to draw from each other's lips. The intense truth and purity of her nature gave to them a poetry which, perhaps, they might have lacked in words.

They were conversing together a few days after he had proposed, and he ventured to touch on what is rather dangerous ground to most lovers—the existence or non-existence of a former affection.

'Am I the first you ever really loved?' he asked; his man's vanity, or curiosity, or whatever it was, indifferent to the possibility of a similar question being put to him.

There was none of that coquettish hesitation that most girls assume when their hearts are analysed thus, as she answered, 'Yes; you are really and truly the very first.'

'I fancied once,' he said, 'that you were not altogether indifferent to Ollinski, but I suppose I must have been wrong.'

'I did not dislike the prince,' she replied, thoughtfully. 'He was so superior to the ordinary men I met, that I had grown rather to think of him as a probable husband; but I knew I did not love him (there was a slight blush here) when I met you.'

'And did you love me from the first?' he asked, fondly.

'Nay,' she replied, with a smile, 'it would be a fasehood were I to flatter you so far as that. I regarded you, perhaps, in another light than a mere stranger when we first met, but love—that is to say true love—is not of such rapid growth. The flower that is forced fades in a few hours ; that which nature rears with her own hand endures its proper term.'

'A flower is a bad simile, I fear,' he said, gravely, 'for, forced or not, they both perish soon. Love should rather resemble the ever-green, or the deathless ivy.'

'I forgot I was talking to a poet,' she answered, laughingly. 'I must be particular when I venture on comparisons next time. But I care not to what you resemble my love, so that it be the emblem of truth and constancy.'

'Nothing better than the ivy,' he said gaily, 'that lives through all seasons, and looks bright and fresh, in spite of storms, and winds, and rains. Am I right, Maud ? Could your love survive in life what it does in nature—peril, adversity, wrong ?'

'The first two I would smile at,' she answered, quickly. 'I would forgive wrong, too, save that it were of that deep and deadly nature which no woman could pardon. Harsh-ness, unkindness, I would excuse, if penitence followed ; but for faithlessness I would have no pity. Were I wronged thus, I would put it beyond my husband's power to wound me again.'

'And would his unworthiness kill your love ? '

'Yes, and no,' she replied. 'I could not love him after, but the love which I bore him before his injustice I could not crush out of my heart. I should love his memory, and look upon himself as dead, even as we treasure a picture of the departed, knowing our kisses and our tears cannot bring them to warmth again.'

'You are a wonderful character, Maud,' he said, admiringly; 'even your pride is nobler than that of ordinary women.'

'I wonder,' he said, presently, 'that you have never asked me the same question I put to you—if I have ever loved before.'

A painful flush rose to her cheek : it was a flush of pride.

'I have never asked you, dearest,' she answered, 'because there is some curiosity whose gratification is fraught with pain. I am sensible enough to imagine that another or others must have had some influence over your heart before you knew me, and I am also just enough not to feel hurt at it; but I am a sufficiently true woman to dislike hearing from your own lips a confirmation of my suspicions.'

He bent over her, and kissed her fondly.

'My darling,' he said, gently, 'whatever boyish dreams or fancies I may have had, there were no women that could have awakened more bright and glowing ones than you. Had I known you first, my heart would never have strayed, even in thought, to another.'

She thanked him with a bright smile.

'At any rate,' she said, 'we are all in all to each other now, whatever ties were formed in the past.'

At the end of a fortnight Carnmore and his betrothed, with her mother and father, left Richmond for London. The Earl of Ravensworth was especially pleased with the result of the visit. He liked Carnmore very much, and he appreciated his niece more than any member of her family. He knew far more of her tastes and sympathies than either Mr. or Mrs. Hilton, and he considered it a most desirable match. 'You love him!' he had whispered to his niece when he first received the announcement, and her answer dispelled any doubt of her indifference.

There were two visits Carnmore intended to pay on his arrival in town, one to Saville, the other to Edith, to officially communicate the news that had, no doubt, reached her from other sources of information. I think an engagement must be telegraphed immediately it is contracted, for a man's friends know it almost as soon as he does himself. He called at his friend's lodgings first, but Saville had left town for a few days. He procured his address, and wrote him a letter in the course of the day acquainting him with what had happened down at Richmond.

His next duty was to see Edith. She had taken matters so sensibly last time that he did not apprehend an unpleasant interview; but, still, it was rather an uncomfortable task to tell a woman with whom he had had such passionate love-passages that he was about to marry another. Still, as it was to be done, it had better be got over at once; so he sallied forth to the Earl of Ardross's residence.

She received him quietly and cordially, yet, there was a somewhat conscious air about her that told she was not in ignorance.

'Have you heard, or is it a piece of news, that '—— he said.

'I have heard,' she answered, interrupting him. 'You and Miss Hilton are too important for your doings to be long kept from the world. I congratulated you when you went down—you scarcely need me to go over the ceremony again.'

He shook his head. There was no petulance or anger in her tone, but rather a deep, uncomplaining sorrow, as of a woman who had learned to steel herself against an impending blow, but on whose powers of endurance it nevertheless told heavily.

'It may seem unjust to you that I have done it,' he said, presently; 'but it was hard to know what to do for the best. God knows, had you been free, there would have been little doubt of my choice.'

'I do not blame you; indeed I do not,

Fred, dear,' she answered, earnestly. 'I know you loved me very dearly, and I repaid your love with wrong. I set the example of faith-lessness. I cannot expect you to be true to a woman who can never reward you.'

'I was beginning to feel very desolate,' he said. 'A man ought not to live like a hermit, shutting himself out from all domestic ties and affections, and going down to the grave unregretted, save by one woman, who dare not weep for him, lest her husband should see her tears, and reproach her for her weakness.'

She was silent at that: perhaps she felt the truth of it. Her love was guilty, and her moan, when it was made, must be made in secret and in trembling, lest others should read her heart.

'It is but just,' she murmured, presently. 'From the bottom of my heart I wish you every happiness. May she make you a better wife than I fear I should have ever done; and though you are another's, and my memory may fade in time, yet, believe me, Fred, I shall always have a deep love left for you. If ever you are in sorrow and trouble, and those

whose place should be by your side have left
you alone, you will yet find a comforter in her
whose heart, as a child or a woman, has been
all your own.'

He wrung her hand fervently, and said—

' A thousand thanks, Edith ; but it almost
unmans me to, hear you talk like that, for it
makes me curse more than ever the gulf that
stretches between us.'

' It is no use repining, dear,' she answered,
gently ; ' let us make the best, not the worst,
of our fate.'

' You will come to the wedding, I suppose ?'
he asked, presently.

' I am afraid I must,' she replied. ' You
will be obliged to invite us, and it might
seem strange to Guy if I made an excuse.'

' Appearances must be kept up, or Mrs.
Grundy would fall foul of us,' he said, rather
bitterly.

He stayed for some time longer, but there
was a restraint on both sides. There was a
wordless sorrow written on Edith's face that
was very legible to him, and he left her house
with far different feelings to those with which

the successful lover of a celebrated beauty is generally credited.

'When I am away I can forget her for a time,' he said to himself, as he took his way to Maud Hilton's; 'but the sound of her voice, the touch of her hand, recalls the spell, and makes me feel as desolate as ever. The new love was baptised in the tears of the old: I fear it was a fatal omen.'

CHAPTER XIV.

'A PROMISE.'

IT was the next day after Carnmore's visit to Edith; he was just preparing to go out when Saville was announced. They shook hands as usual, but there was an abruptness and restlessness in the manner of the latter that did not escape his friend.

'I see you are going out,' he said, in an unusually curt, constrained voice, 'but I will not detain you long. I received your letter telling me of your engagement to Maud Hilton. Not a year ago you were so passionately in love with Lady Ardross, that you would have hesitated at no obstacle to work her own and her husband's dishonour. How am I to reconcile that with the fact you announce?'

Carnmore's brow darkened, and he answered haughtily—

'Your tone is somewhat dictatorial; more so than even our close friendship would warrant. I am not aware of any right that would empower you to *demand* an explanation of my conduct. If I choose to offer one that is a different matter.'

'Tush!' answered Saville, impatiently— 'the result is the same, whether I demand or you volunteer. It is scarcely worth while splitting straws as to the difference between the means of obtaining it.'

Saville's manner was a perfect enigma to his friend, but he judged it best to humour him, in order to arrive at some solution of the matter, so he said, calmly—

'As you say, it is not a year ago I loved Edith Stewart passionately. Were she free now, I have little doubt I should love her passionately still ; but, as it is, I have learned to see the folly of giving my love to a woman who cannot reward it, and have chosen some one who can bestow her heart in exchange for mine.'

'Do you love Maud Hilton as deeply as you loved your cousin?' questioned Saville, briefly and sternly.

Again Hammersley's brow darkened—his friend's tone was too inquisitorial.

'I must repeat again, Saville,' he answered, 'that I fail to recognise your right to analyse my private feelings thus. My taking or not taking a wife can be a matter of small interest to you.'

'A matter of small interest to me!' repeated Saville, with a sharp pain in his tones that smote his listener's ear uncomfortably. 'It is in this case a matter of vital import. The passionate love you knew for Edith Stewart, and which I will stake my life on it you do not know for Maud Hilton, has found an echo in my heart. The woman who has accepted you for her husband is the same at whose feet I laid the hopes of my life. I loved her madly up to the hour that her own lips dispelled my dreams; but my love has outlived the rejection which would have killed that of less intense natures, and I worship her madly still. Can you doubt, after that, whether this mad passion gives me a right to demand of the man who marries Maud Hilton if he will cherish her as I would have cherished—if he loves her with the love that has made a shipwreck and a hideous dream of my life ? '

Had a thunderbolt fallen at his feet, Carnmore could not have been more astonished. It was strange ; but although he had known, to some extent, of their intimacy, he had never associated their names together in anything but friendship.

'You loved Maud Hilton !' he said, presently. 'Why, why did you never tell me of it long ago ? '

'Why !' echoed Saville, impatiently. 'Say, rather, why should I ? Is it such a pleasant sensation for a man to pour the details of his rejection on a friend's ears? Was I to whine and cry like a child who sees his house of cards tumble down before his eyes ? '

'Had you told me this,' answered Hammersley, scarcely heeding his friend's last speech, 'I would never have become your rival ; I would have avoided her while it was time.'

'I didn't expect that of you or any man living,' replied Saville, in the same impatient tone. 'I am not such a selfish or unjust fool as to begrudge everybody else the possession of what I cannot win for myself. You are pledged to Maud Hilton, and if she loves you, as I believe she must, or she would not marry you, God grant she may never repent her choice. But I ask you, as man to man, as one who has known your past history, Is your love for her worthy the truth and purity she brings to your arms ? '

There was a long pause before Hammersley answered that direct question. At length he spoke :

'I will answer you frankly, Saville, as frankly as I would have a man answer me, did I love like you, and he were my rival. I do not love Maud with the mad passion I knew for Edith, but I love her with a nobler and, I trust, a more steadfast love—a love that increases in strength every day I become more acquainted with her pure and earnest nature ; and I can promise you solemnly that, as far as it lays in my power, Maud Hilton shall never repent her choice.'

'It is as I thought,' answered Saville, gloomily. 'If your first love was as intense as mine, as I believe it was, it is a mockery to offer your heart to another woman. It is too late to alter it now, for, I doubt not, she is fascinated too deeply to go back ; but, mark what I say, if there ever comes an hour when Maud Hilton has to complain of wrong from you, I will constitute myself her avenger, and, were it my own brother at whose hands I sought the reparation due to her, I would not rest till I had exacted the debt in full. We have been friends, Carnmore, and, wherever we meet, we will be friends still ; but I cannot enter the house, nor sit at the table, where her presence revives a bitter memory. Farewell, till we meet where that can never be a subject of contention between us ; but remember the task to which I have pledged myself.'

He wrung his friend's hand, and was gone before he could utter a word.

CHAPTER XV.

'A FRESH PAGE.'

CARNMORE took his way to the house of his betrothed, pondering deeply over his interview with Saville. Here, at last, was the solution of that mysterious change which he had noticed in him on the first night of his arrival in town. He could scarcely wonder that he had chosen to make a secret of his love. No man likes to relate the story of an unsuccessful wooing, even to his dearest friend. There had been little humiliation in Carnmore's confidence. Edith Stewart had loved him dearly once. His was no history of deliberate rejection, and he, therefore, did not feel hurt to think his friend had declined to entrust him with the secret of his heart. But, nevertheless, he felt troubled for Saville : he knew his deep and sterling character, and felt sure that it was no mere boyish worship of a fair face that had awakened his heart from its long sleep. It distressed him to think that, after such confidence and friendship as rarely exists between two men, he should at last prove his rival in a matter so dear. True that Saville had been rejected before he had appeared on the scene, and he had his own word for it that he was not unreasonable enough to hate the man who succeeded in winning what he could not ; but, still, it is always harder to see a thing we cherish pass into the possession of a friend than into that of an utter stranger. Besides, Saville was so well acquainted with his passion for Edith, a passion which he could not confidently assert to himself was thorougly conquered. He hoped to crush it out of his heart in time, but at present it was still there, ever watchful and. wakeful.

He could not help contrasting the nobleness of Saville's love with that of ordinary men, nay, even with what his own' had been under the same circumstances. His only anxiety was

that another should love Maud as devotedly
as he.   The wishes of most rejected lovers
tend in the opposite direction.   Disappointment is seldom charitable to others' success;
and he could not help wondering that such a
nature should have been incapable of waking
an appreciative love in Maud's bosom.   But
he almost directly found an answer to this in
his own heart.   He was fully aware of the
superiority of Maud in point of character over
Edith ; yet, how well he knew that the most
passionate love was given to the least worthy.
It is idle wondering why or wherefore in
regard to human passions : they are things
of mere caprice, and reason has little or no
sovereignty over them.

It was not long before he tabled the subject
to Maud.

'I have an accusation to prefer against
you,' he said, with a smile.

'Indeed!' she answered, looking at him
unconcernedly.   'Now, see what it is to have
a clear conscience.   Had I done any great
wrong, I should be blushing and looking
guilty ; as it is, I know I am perfectly inno-

cent, and have no fear of anything that is coming.'

'Oh, it is not a very awful charge,' he said, gaily; 'so there would be no necessity to be disturbed about it in either case. All I have to accuse you of is a little reticence.'

'Reticence!' she repeated, in a surprised tone; 'I do not understand you. What is it I have been concealing from you?'

'You have not been quite explicit in the names and numbers of all your admirers,' he said, with a slight smile.

'It were an endless task to recapitulate the list of *all* my adorers,' she answered, gaily. 'But what special omission have you discovered to-day?'

'I never knew Saville proposed to you,' he replied.

A grave and rather pained look came for·a moment over her face at that name.

'I never told you about him, Fred, dearest,' she answered, 'because he was too sincere a wooer to have his rejection made a boast of, even to you; and, moreover, I could not altogether acquit myself of some blame in the matter.'

'You lured him on, I suppose?' he questioned, with a smile. 'A man like him was a mighty captive to drag at your car.'

'No, indeed,' she said, earnestly. 'You do me injustice. I made use of no arts to attach him to me. But the facts of our acquaintance were simply these: I was attracted by his evident talent and depth of character the first night we met. It was so delightful to find some congenial mind among the petty intellects by whom I was surrounded, that I became great friends with him without thinking, at the time, that my apparent preference for his society might lead him to suppose I prized it from another motive. I discovered, too late, that he had so far misinterpreted my conduct as to entertain a deep and sincere love. I tried, when I found this, to avoid him as much as possible; but, one day, at a garden party of my uncle's, he proposed formally. I had, of course, nothing to give but refusal; but it is always a painful episode in my life.

because I consider he is too noble and good to have to love in vain.'

'He evidently loved you passionately,' replied Carnmore, seriously; 'for I had a visit from him myself to-day, in consequence of the letter I had sent to him announcing our engagement. He questioned me very sternly and searchingly as to the depth of my own love for you, and concluded by promising that, if ever you had to complain of wrong at my hands, he would constitute himself your avenger, and exact from me the utmost reparation.'

'Poor fellow!' said Maud, sadly. 'I had hoped he would have forgotten me by this time, or, at any rate, that the wound had healed somewhat; but I suppose he is like me— where love has once been he cannot put forgetfulness in its place.'

Carnmore bent down and kissed her very fondly.

'My darling Maud,' he said, 'I, too, am deeply sorry for this infatuation of Saville's, for he was my friend, and I esteemed him as much as you possibly could. I regret, more than anything, that it is I who must prove his rival, although I know he is too just to blame me for doing what he could not help—falling in love with you. But I can promise this : he shall never have cause to despise, though he cannot help envying, your husband.'

The days of their engagement rapidly sped on, and the wedding was fixed for the month of February. Many guests were bidden, among the rest Lord and Lady Ardross. Carnmore had not seen much of Edith during his betrothal : he knew her power over him too well to venture often within its reach. Three days before his marriage he was walking down Portland Place, when he met his cousin's carriage. She pulled the check-string, and beckoned to him to come to the window.'

'Guy has been taken ill with a slight cold and fever at Luton, where he went down on Wednesday to look after some local business ; and I am going down to him now. He will be sure not to be well enough to come to your wedding, and I shall stay with him ; so you will not see me either.'

'Very well,' he said, gravely ; 'I cannot

candidly say I shall be sorry at your absence. There is only one way in which I should have ever liked to see you at my wedding, and that was as a bride. Since that cannot be, it is better so.'

'Much,' she answered, sadly. 'Good-bye, Freddy darling—it is the last time I shall address you so affectionately as that; and, from the bottom of my heart, I wish you happiness.'

That was the last time he saw her before his marriage, but those simple words haunted him even at his wedding feast.

Saville, of course, did not come: he had requested Carnmore previously not to invite him. But there was a brilliant company to make amends for the two who had painful reasons for their absence. Bride and bridegroom alike were remembered regretfully that day in two hearts.

It had been dull all the morning up to the time when they drove away. As they turned the corner that shut Mr. Hilton's house from view the sun darted out brilliantly from the sombre clouds which had kept it captive so long.

'Look, darling,' said Maud, smiling, as she touched her husband's arm to bid him observe the fortunate omen ; 'shall not that be typical of the brightness of our lives for henceforth and for ever ?'

He drew her closely towards him in a fond embrace, as he answered gravely—

'God grant no shadow may ever darken its brightness.'

As he spoke, the dark dull clouds swept again over the sun, as if in very defiance to his prayer. Maud shuddered slightly, but said, with a cheerful smile—

'Our lives are what we choose to make them ; they do not depend upon portents and omens.'

But her husband was not so easily comforted. He was rather superstitious, and that slight event had affected him unfavourably.

'Our lives are what we choose to make them,' he thought sadly to himself. 'I fear me, not always. Hitherto, I think, fate alone has had the ordering of my destiny.'

CHAPTER XVI.

'AFTER MARRIAGE.'

THE 'merry month of May' found Lord and Lady Carnmore in town again, with the rest of their acquaintance. Three moons had waned since their marriage, but I don't think their love had grown any less. Certainly it had not on her side, and, with regard to himself, he found that the longer he knew Maud the greater was the probability of finding something fresh to render her more lovable in his eyes. There was no paltry pride in her: if she disliked anything in her husband's conduct she told him of it frankly, and thought it better to do so than nurse her grievances in silence, as many proud and sensitive women take such a morbid delight in doing.

And Carnmore began to feel that she was

getting very dear to him, becoming loved with
a love that was for herself, not for her beauty
or other mere extraneous recommendations.
It is true there was not the passion in her
that a man of his romantic temperament rather
expected.   Maud was not a woman who could
love voluptuously.   There was a tranquillity
about her affection which contrasted strangely
with the remembrance of that other image
which he had not utterly succeeded yet in
banishing from his heart.   Maud would meet
him after a short absence with a bright smile,
and wind her arms gently and caressingly
round his neck, with a soft kiss or two ; Edith
would have sprung eagerly into his arms,
and have given him a spontaneous shower of
kisses unasked.   I am afraid, after all, most
men like to be loved in this manner.   Who
does not prefer the roughness and the fresh-
ness of the ocean to the calm, shining waters
of the lake, although those latter may be by
far the safest on which to adventure our
barque ?

But I think the great bond of love between
Carnmore and his wife was her thorough

sympathy with his tastes and pursuits. She so revered intellect in others that she positively adored it in her husband. Night after night would she sit by his side, as he prepared his speeches, or as he composed his poems, her eyes sparkling with anticipated triumph to think how the verdict of the world should confirm her own estimate of his genius. Edith was somewhat different from this. Where she loved she exalted the object into a god; and, had he been the greatest dolt in creation she would still have believed his utterances superior to those of other men. That other people should think as highly of him as she thought was, therefore, of little moment to her. This arose, perhaps, from a total absence of ambition in her, save connected with the one aim and object of her life. Her sole ambition was that she should be loved by her lover as devotedly and passionately as she loved him. The praise of others, other occupations, other desires than those of love, seemed so many rivals for her place in his heart.

It was a selfish love, this of Edith's, I know; such a love, as persisted in by many women and yielded to by many men, would go far to render life a very useless and unprofitable possession. Fortunately, such passionate natures are rare. With all woman-kind love is a religion; but, with comparatively few, a fanaticism. And Carnmore thoroughly gauged the difference between the two women. He knew that Maud might love him for himself now, but that still the first attraction in her eyes had been his intellect, the admiration for which had preceded her love; and he knew that Edith had loved him in her childish days because such love had seemed natural to her, not because of extraneous qualities that, commencing with demanding, end by winning it.

But still, though he could not pretend to himself that he could ever love Maud with the mad, wild passion he had known for Edith, he was beginning to look upon the latter as dead to him, and to bury the old love with the rest of that past that slept, white and cold, its grave only marked by the flowers and *immortelles* of memory. Could no change have taken place in their relations for two or three years, I believe he could have never brought back that old love to life, any more than manhood would be able to take delight in the toys which amused its infancy. I believe, had Maud and Edith both been free then, his heart, fortified by reason, would have elected the former. But fate had ordered it otherwise.

His acquaintance with Saville might be virtually said to have ceased. He came across him very rarely in society, and there was a constraint between them that it seemed impossible to dispel. Carnmore had tried to break the ice one night, when he had accidentally met him in the lobby of the House of Commons; but Saville's demeanour, although it implied no resentment or dislike, sufficiently indicated that their friendly relations could never be renewed.

'It is such ages since I met you,' Carnmore had remarked, cordially, in the hope that it might draw from his old friend some tacit acknowledgment of regret at their separation.

Saville had replied coldly and briefly; and Carnmore, rather hurt, said—

'I am sorry to think my marriage has lost me a man whose friendship I had reckoned among the few things to be proud of in this world; but I suppose we cannot enjoy everything at once. Great wealth in one portion of the community implies great poverty in another; and, if a man is rich in love, I expect he must be content to be impoverished in friendship.'

There was something in his tone that touched Saville, for he answered, less constrainedly—

'You ought to make some allowance for my avoidance of you, Carnmore. I remember our friendship as tenderly as you. It is because I would not have other feelings supply the place of tenderness that I cross your path as little as possible. I have told you that I am not paltry or unreasonable enough to hate you because you won what I could not; but, still, I am a man with somewhat of human nature's weaknesses and injustice in my human composition; and were I to be always with you, and consequently be reminded of the fact that you are my successful rival in *her* heart, I don't know how long it might be before I began to dislike my old friend.'

'Since needs be, it must then,' answered Carnmore, gloomily.

'Never repine, man,' answered Saville, more cheerfully. 'When man is fed to surfeiting with love, what need has he of such a coarse and gross viand as friendship? You are a strange lover if Maud cannot compensate you for every other omission of life.'

They were getting on rather delicate ground here, so Carnmore thought it time to bid his friend adieu. He did so regretfully, knowing that it was indeed a real farewell; for he had thoroughly enjoyed friendship with Saville. So many of their ideas and tastes had been in common, that it seemed it would prove a long time ere he found another companion whose nature would be so congenial to his own.

'I must have been born under a most evil star,' he thought to himself, as he walked home after that interview. 'Everything in which I have been mixed up has turned out disastrously. I loved at first, as I thought, in vain ; yet I meet her when married, and I learn she loves me still. I fall in love a second time, and I must needs prove a rival to the man who has been my dearest friend. I seem to have encountered nothing but storms and perils hitherto. I wonder if, in truth, I have reached a haven at last.'

I believe he was right. There seem some people who act as if they were the blindest of instruments in the hands of fate—men, whose headlong and tempestuous passions hurry them to the extremes of misfortune, and often of wrong-doing ; men, in whose morning of life there may be a few gleams of triumph, even the triumph of successful wrong-doing ; but on whose evening too surely steals the footsteps of the insulted Nemesis, leaving them gazing with despairing eyes and blasted heart on the waste of waters, on whose fair bosom rode for a time the proud and stately barque that carried their hopes only to be wrecked with their happiness, and that of all they loved on board.

CHAPTER XVII.

'TOO LATE.'

WHAT a memorable epoch did it commence in his life, that July morning on which he entered his cousin's house to luncheon, by an invitation given him by Ardross himself the day previously. He found Lady Allerton and Florence in the drawing-room with Edith. The former welcomed him very warmly, and the conversation grew so general and animated that the time appointed by Ardross for luncheon was past by several minutes before anyone observed it.

'How late Guy is,' remarked Edith, carelessly, 'and generally he is so very punctual. Besides, he asked Fred to come himself. I can't understand what detains him.'

Florence rose and walked to the window, probably to discover a glimpse of the tardy earl. All at once they saw her turn deadly pale, and clutch the chair next her convulsively. He then advanced towards her to learn the cause of that sudden emotion. It was not far to seek. A cab was at the door, and two men were carrying in the body of the Earl of Ardross, with a handkerchief thrown over his face.

They saw and guessed its terrible import in a second. Edith gave an awful, shuddering cry, and fell into her mother's arms, while Carnmore hastened down into the hall, where the servants, with scared looks and white faces, had already gathered.

He learned the explanation in a few words from the groom who had attended his master in his ride. The horse on which Ardross had been mounted was a fiery young chesnut, recently purchased, exceedingly nervous, and violently addicted to shying. A huge waggon, suddenly turning the corner, had raised his dangerous proclivities, and, without the least warning, he had flung his rider heavily on to the kerbstone. Some passers-by hastened to him immediately, but he was quite dead. They took him to the nearest doctor, but he was beyond the reach of medical skill.

They bore him silently up the wide staircase, which he had descended a few hours before strong in the strength of health and youth, helpless and feeble now, in the stern embrace of his grim conqueror, Death. What a satire did it seem on human vanity, that still, impotent corpse! Yesterday, it had been bowed down to and worshipped on account of the wealth it could call its own, of the titles and honours in which it clothed itself; to-day, it was a lump of lifeless clay, differing in nought from the humblest beggar whose rags fluttered in the winds!

Carnmore went back to the drawing-room. Edith was standing there, with a strange, stony look in her dark, bright eyes.

'You must let me go to him at once,' she said, earnestly—'I do not fear death. I did not shrink from him living. My place is by his side till they take him from me.'

He led her gently up to the bed on which

they had placed him, her mother and sister following. The livid, unearthly pallor—that ashy hue of death whose peculiar tint no artist's hand can reproduce—had settled over his face; but, when one looked at the firm, stalwart limbs—the clear, calm features, without a wrinkle or other sign of age, it seemed hard that he should be thus stricken down in the pride of youth and strength, ere even his manhood had reached its prime.

She bent down and kissed the mute lips, from which some would have recoiled with a strange feeling of dread, and then presently the tears came gushing forth, as they will in all sorrow, save in that stony despair too deep, too intense for tears.

. 'Oh, Guy, darling!' she wailed, piteously; 'to think you should leave me without one last word, one last look; without your head being pillowed on the bosom of her you loved so well!'

It was no fierce, unnatural grief she felt, no deep and awful loss that could never be replaced henceforth. She had loved the dead man who had slept by her side, whose name she had borne ; but it was not a love that would make the light go out of her life when he was gone ; and, perhaps, at that moment, her sense of the great difference between his love for her and hers for him smote her reproachfully, for she cried, presently—

'I did not love you, dearest, as you loved me. I had but little heart to give you, for it had been broken ere I married ; but I tried to make a good and faithful wife to you, and would have kept so in spite of temptation.'

Carnmore put his arm caressingly round her.

'Hush, Edith, dear,' he said, gently : 'no one is accusing you. I am sure *he* never blamed you in aught.'

'Oh, Fred,' she cried, wildly, 'it is no use pretending to conceal the truth. Mamma knew, Florence knew, I married him without the love I ought to have had for him—the love every wife should bear the man she calls husband ; and I was guilty in so doing. I prevented him from finding another woman who could have loved him as he deserved.'

Lady Allerton attempted to utter some soothing words, but her widowed daughter turned from her impatiently.

'I know what you would say,' she cried, impetuously : 'that other girls would have married him for his wealth and position, which, I take God to witness, were no object in my eyes. I married him because I liked him, because I thought that in time I should learn to love him ; and perhaps I should, had the temptation of my old love never been put in my way again.'

It was impossible to silence her. The pent-up emotions of those years since her parting with Carnmore—the remorse—the remembrance of her struggles between conscience and duty—all found vent now. Pride was forgotten in the awful presence of Death.

' He was goodness itself to me,' she went on, presently. ' He never asked a question of my past, never breathed a suspicion of my present; but I know, if he has learned all in that world to which he has gone, he must reproach me now with faithlessness to him in heart, although I kept myself pure in deed.'

Again Carnmore tried to stem the tide of these bitter self-accusations.

'Edith,' he said, gently, 'you are indeed blaming yourself without cause. Ardross could not have expected you to volunteer to him the history of your heart. He took you for what he found you, and, no doubt, was quite contented. You must not let your morbid sensitiveness convert him into a deeply-wronged man.'

That appeal aroused a new phase in her distraught emotion. She rose from the side of her dead husband, and clung hysterically to her cousin, heedless of the fact that her mother and sister were there as witnesses of her utter abnegation of pride.

'You will stay with me in my grief, Fred dear, will you not?' she said, pleadingly. 'You will not leave me to bear this reproach by myself. You know you have to bear some blame in it as well. Had it not been for you, I might have come to him with a pure and unsullied heart. Had it not been for your presence in my married life, I might have learned to think of none but him. You will

stay with me, Fred dear—your wife cannot
mind. I have a claim on you before her.
She has loved you for months, I have loved
you for years. She has you bound firmly to
her now : she cannot begrudge a few moments
to your old love—to the woman who was your
playmate in childhood, whose pride and folly
gave you such bitter pain. You shall go to
her after that for ever ; you shall put me for
henceforth out of your life ; and I will go away
alone to pray for you and my poor Guy, whom
I married only to *piqué* you.'

She laid her head on his shoulder, and wept
bitterly and piteously. Carnmore laid his
lips lightly on hers ; and, turning to Lady
Allerton, said, sadly—

'You have learned our secret at last, aunt.
A fatal quarrel separated us, to make both our
lives miserable hereafter. We met again, and
knew we loved as madly as ever ; but, standing here in the solemn presence of death, I
declare to you that she has been innocent of
what the world calls wrong to her husband.
Faithless in thought she may have been, but
his honour has been safe in her keeping ;

otherwise she could scarcely bear to look upon him now.'

Lady Allerton made no reply, but the tears rolled heavily down her cheeks as she watched the prostrate figure of her daughter clinging to the man who was her husband in heart, if the other had been her rightful one in name.

She crossed over, and unwound her arms gently, and led her to a chair, and held her tenderly to her bosom, while Florence knelt at her feet, sobbing all the while.

It was a mournful scene : the dead man lying there, unconscious, in the serenity of his deep and abiding sleep, of the bitter tears and self-accusations of the wife in whose love he had so believed ; and the man who had been his deadliest rival—his rivalry undreamt of—standing by his bed, and gazing on him with a strange feeling of remorse! It was but a few months ago that he had said to himself—'Death alone can unbind the chains forged by her pride and folly ; ' and lo, the hand of Death had snapped them ! It seemed a dream to him to know that Edith was free—that she could love him without sin.

And, then, as he stood gazing on those calm, pale features—on those mute lips that could never demand faith or obedience more—there rose before his eyes the image of Maud, in all her tranquil and seraphic beauty, and, with a strange shudder and shiver at his heart, he muttered to himself—' Too late, too late ! '

CHAPTER XVIII.

'FREE.'

THE Earl of Ardross was borne to his last resting-place with all the pomp and pageantry with which the world delights to honour her wealthy dead; and, in a few weeks, Edith recovered from the grief which had had its origin rather in an undefined sense of remorse than in any real tenderness for her departed husband. Time cures the deepest and most painful wounds. It is scarcely probable that mere bruises and flesh-cuts will long resist its healing influence. Kind and loving women forget their helpmeets in so far as union with another implies forgetfulness; and Ardross soon slept in his early grave, not utterly forgotten, but, certainly, unbewailed, by his widow. He was the second man who had died whose love for her had assumed the form of a worship. But what memory could she have for dead loves when that one living one absorbed all her heart? Such were but the landmarks of her life-journey—the goal lay as yet far stretched into infinite space.

The sudden death of Ardross had awoke an utter revulsion of feeling in Carnmore's breast. Once more the image of Edith stole across his dreams, surrounded with all the beauty and fascination with which the ardour of his first passion had invested her. A little time before, and he could not have acknowledged to himself that Edith now occupied the first place in his heart. Maud was so much more worthy, in many respects, to her rival, and, certainly, so indisputably her equal in physical gifts, that he had, now and then, fancied he would not have changed his past life, even had the change given him Edith in those early days when he so passionately loved her. But now, the knowledge that she was free, free to be his own had he not fettered himself so firmly, awoke once more the mad, wild passion that had made such wild work with his heart.

I believe true love never dies. Pride, anger, reason, may crush it down in our hearts for a time, and we blindly imagine it dead; we may bind it, as we think, in adamantine chains, and laugh to ourselves with triumph, to know that it is manacled and powerless; but let us sleep upon our post for a second; let us remove, no matter for what brief interval, those sentinels under whose watchfulness it writhes, and foams, and pants; and lo! the fetters are burst, and it rises, like a giant from captivity, strong with the passionate strength of life and freedom, mad with the remembrance of its hours of bondage.

He could understand better now that firm refusal of Edith to dishonour her husband when he had pleaded to her to repair the wrong she had inflicted. I believe he loved her now more madly, if possible, than ever. The very restraint imposed upon his passion served the rather to inflame it; but he would not have voluntarily wronged Maud in deed. He had not ceased to love her: he loved her as a man may love his mother, and regret to leave her, yet, nevertheless, goes to the stranger woman whom he has placed before her in his heart ; but he knew that his honour and faith demanded the sacrifice of this unholy lust for another woman ; and one night, when he had felt that old love surging up too wildly in his heart, he had registered a solemn oath never to voluntarily forsake Maud for Edith.

I believe he would have kept that vow to the death had not Maud herself placed him beyond the necessity of observing it. In spite of his good resolutions on the one point, he could not always forego the expression of his guilty love to Edith, and one day it happened that Maud became a listener.

There had never been friendship between the two women, although, of course, considering their near relationship, it was only natural they should visit. Of course, there was sufficient reason why Edith should not like her cousin's wife ; but on Maud's side there was at first no cause for prejudice. Afterwards, I fancy, some hints of the old relations between her husband and Edith must have reached her from some quarters. These little histories are never forgotten in the fashionable world, especially when their revival can make anyone uncomfortable. At any rate, very latterly, she had had considerable misgivings. It was a long time before she indulged them, for she was so pure herself that it was hard at first to suspect impurity in others. But when she once admitted the probability of her suspicions, a hundred little circumstances, scarcely perhaps observed at the time, but fraught with deep significance when brought into conjunction with that assumed data, confirmed her doubts. It was a terrible trial to her proud nature to suspect baseness in the idol she had believed so immaculate; but she was not a woman to shrink from the duty of vindicating her own dignity, although it was doubly hard that it should be outraged by one so near and dear to her.

It was at the close of the season, and the Duchess of Featherstone gave a grand garden party, to which none but the cream of London society was invited. It was little more than a year since Ardross's death, and this was almost the first large gathering at which Edith had been present.

Carnmore and Maud went together, but, of course, soon separated on their arrival. He met his cousin shortly, and they strolled about together for some time. The grounds of the Duchess of Featherstone abounded with little out-of-the-way nooks and corners, and they were not long in finding one of these harbours of refuge.

Maud had soon grown weary of the gay scene, and went in search of her husband, little dreaming that she should detect him so speedily in flagrant infidelity. She sauntered carelessly along, till she was arrested by the sound of voices talking low and earnestly. She paused, for one of the voices sounded marvellously like that of Edith Ardross. Unfortunately, she was not deceived. The next instant her clear tones rang out on the air, unconscious that there was an interested listener so near.

These were the words that Maud heard her speak—

'It is a mockery for you to speak of love.

Have you not quoted your wife to me as nothing short of perfection since the hour when you were first fascinated with her insipid beauty? Do you not din me incessantly with the boast of your constancy to her? I know you would never leave her for me. Why are you constantly implying that I demand such a sacrifice any more than I ask for your love?'

An awful pain tightened round Maud's heart, for her instinct told her whose voice she would recognise in the reply before those deep, earnest tones she knew so well, placed it beyond doubt.

'Why?' he answered. 'Because I can read your woman's heart at last—because, when I asked you a certain question, years ago, in Paris, you told me you would have had no scruple for yourself, but only for your husband's honour. I know you love me well enough to envy my being another's. I love you well enough to wish I could rend my fetters without disloyalty to the woman whose pure and unsullied nature I do reverence to. But I cannot, Edith; I am bound for life.

Were I free, I would lay everything in the world at your feet.'

He bent over her when he had finished, and pressed his eager, passionate lips to hers. Suddenly, in the midst of that caress, he felt Edith tremble violently, and, looking up, saw the eyes of his outraged wife fixed upon the pair.

He cowered and shrunk before the contemptuous, searching gaze of the woman who had hitherto never looked on him save with tenderness.

'Lady Ardross,' she said, coldly and distinctly—never had her beauty seemed so superb as when she stood there gazing, like a stern judge, on the guilty pair before her— 'your lover is free from the fetters which his own hands were the first to bind. You loved him first. You have a prior claim to the woman whom he made his wife, because he lost you. He seems to think he must make a heavy sacrifice to enable him to come to your arms. I only ask you one thing—let your love be such that it can reward him for all he rejects for your sake.'

Edith made no reply; she still continued to tremble violently. Carnmore was the first to recover himself; but he could not meet the gaze of his outraged wife, as he answered, hesitatingly—

'Maud, come with me away from here, and I will offer you the best explanation of this most unfortunate scene.'

Maud turned haughtily on him at that, and her eyes literally blazed with scorn, as she said—

'You mistake the woman with whom you have to deal, Lord Carnmore. Do you remember me telling you once that my love would forgive all save the deep and deadly wrong that is an insult to love? I little thought, when I told you so, that an hour should ever come that would prove my firmness; but it has come, without my seeking, and the fittest explanation that can be offered is to be found here, in the attitude in which I found you, in the passionate regrets that I heard you utter.'

Again he attempted to speak, but she stopped him with an imperious gesture.

'Stay,' she said, haughtily, 'do not attempt
to put a false interpretation upon this scene.
I know your gift of language well, but in
this instance it will fail you.   Hereafter, if
you have a spark of manhood left, you must
blush at the degradation to which I was
witness ; you must blush to remember that
I looked upon you with contempt, and that
you deserved it.   Do not add to that memory
the humiliating thought that you stooped to
lie, and lied in vain.'

There was silence for a moment; it was
broken by Edith.   She advanced close to her
rival, and said, pleadingly, with the heavy
tears rolling down her cheeks :

'You have not deigned to hear his defence :
let me plead for him.   He loved me when
we were children together.   I was betrothed
to him, and I wronged him cruelly.   I married
another, and forbade him to speak of love to
me.   He met you, and he honoured and loved
you.   Nay, do not look so scornfully, I will
swear he did.   Then, when I was free, I was
weak enough to let my love for him appear,
till he fancied that he cared for me as he did

of old. But it is but a fancy on his part; I am sure you are first in his heart. Will you forgive him, and I will promise never to see him again?'

She looked so lovely and gentle in her humiliation, that a softened look involuntarily stole over Maud's face. She said, less harshly—

'If you are one of those miserable women who have sacrificed their life's happiness to their pride, from the bottom of my heart I compassionate you; but for *him*—for the man who wooed me with the emphasis of passion in his voice—who insulted me with the mockery and the simulation of love—I have nought left but loathing and contempt. I loved him, aye, Lady Ardross, as dearly as you do, although I might have been duller in showing it, perhaps, while I believed in him. But now that faith is shattered : I have plucked the love from my heart, never to return again.'

Edith would have spoken again, but she interrupted her.

' One word,' she said, addressing her husband. 'I shall go to my father's directly I

leave here.   Do not think for a moment that
any prayers or entreaties could alter my
resolution.   Were my pride silent, my love
for you is gone, and I could come back to no
man whose nature I despised.'

'I know I have deserved your contempt,'
he said, in a hollow voice.

'Farewell!' she said, as she turned from
that spot where a great shadow had darkened
over her life.   'Could I bring a union between
you and the woman you love—could I spare
her the dishonour she must otherwise reap in
coming to you—I would, but it is not in my
power.   May this be your last infidelity.   Do
not repay her love with the treachery which
you have extended to mine.'

She turned away with those words, and left
the man who had been her husband—who was
her husband still in the eyes of the world—
alone with her rival.   The sun was shining
brightly, scarcely a cloud to be detected in the
clear empyrean, as she walked slowly back
from that spot where she had learned such a
bitter truth.

Suddenly, the incongruity of the brilliant

scene around with her own desolate feelings struck her keenly. She gazed up at the cloudless heavens with a weary, heart-broken look.

'You lie now,' she said, sadly to herself: 'you smile upon me when you should frown. You told the truth on the day of our marriage; then you were dark and drear, like my life.'

The babble of voices, the rich dresses, the gaiety, the happiness around her, awoke a bitter pain. Henceforth, what was the world to her broken heart? She had been told by many—by the man even who had wronged her so cruelly—that she was superior to ordinary women. Yet it had come to this—that the commonest nature among her own sex could not have been more miserable.

CHAPTER XIX.

'CROSSING THE RUBICON.'

'I AM left now without a home. My own lips have banished the woman who would have ministered faithfully to me, though I could not love her as she deserved. I am beggared in social ties—must I be beggared in love also? Edith, will you reward me now for all I have suffered and lost for your sake?'

So spoke Carnmore, on the next afternoon to that memorable scene, sitting with Edith alone in the Marchioness of Allerton's drawing-room. Maud had gone, as she threatened, direct to her father's on leaving the Duchess of Featherstone's. But sufficient time had not yet elapsed for it to become the common talk of the world, although, no doubt, the news was already beginning to percolate rapidly.

Edith buried her face in her hands, and was silent at that direct appeal. He continued, quickly and earnestly—

'I know you cannot come to me now, without what the world calls dishonour. I would have spared you this, darling, had it lain in my power. I would have waited for years, could I have formed a reasonable expectation that you would be free at the end; but how could I have known that my patience would have been so little taxed?'

She rose and flung her arms passionately round his neck.

'The world is nothing to me without you,' she said, impetuously; 'why should I weigh the world against you?'

He looked up with a great joy in his face.

'You will come, then?' he questioned, eagerly, of her.

Another passionate caress was her answer, and he strained her to his heart in the mad intoxication of triumph.

Suddenly she withdrew herself from his embrace, as if a fresh thought had struck her.

'Fred, darling,' she said, earnestly, 'is it

not right that you should try again to be reconciled to Maud first? She may be more likely to forgive now.'

He shook his head with a sad smile.

' Don't think, because I have not mentioned her name yet, that I feel no remorse on her account. But the Rubicon is passed—my wrong has raised a gulf between us that neither can ever cross to be reconciled. Even could she forgive, I never could obliterate the sense of my humiliation. My sin to her has turned me into a coward : I could not look in her face again.'

' And this has been all my doing,' she moaned, bitterly.

' Nay, Edith,' he answered, gravely ; ' do not blame yourself so utterly. We have loved to our own ruin, and to that of others ; but is was hard for us to say to ourselves—we will not love.'

' I cannot excuse myself so easily,' she said, with a sharp pain in her voice. ' Hitherto, I have proved a curse to all who loved me. I shipwrecked your life years ago, and I am now exiling you from every noble ambition of

life in the future. I have given the woman
who should have been nearest and dearest to
you cause to hate me to the death. I lied in
thought to the man who was my husband
when I stood by his side at the altar ; and I
wrought the death of another by my heedless
love of admiration—by the culpable vanity
that regarded human hearts as playthings to
be won and then tossed aside. God ! how
shall I face my Maker when that dead man,
lying in his self-made grave, rises at the judgment seat, and points to me as his murderess ? '

She had bowed her head upon his bosom,
and was sobbing bitterly.

' Oh, the curse of beauty ! ' she moaned,
sorrowfully. ' Why did not God take me to
himself when I was a little child, when I was
pure and innocent, and might have been fit
for His kingdom ? Why was I left to curse
my guilty and degraded womanhood, to contrast those days with the ones that have slain
my soul to the very death ? '

' Hush, darling ! ' he answered, tenderly.
' You have been proud, and wayward, and
wilful, but these are not errors that will

provoke eternal damnation. You were not to blame for Rochester's mad infatuation, any more than that Ardross chose to take you without asking a question of your past. Our love now is guilty, I doubt not, but I am your partner in the guilt.'

She looked up at him very mournfully, and said—

' Do you know, Fred, that, when I think over all my wickednesses and folly, I wish I were dead ? It is the only atonement I could make.'

He clasped her passionately to his breast.

' Do not talk of death ! ' he said, fearfully ; ' live at least for me now. I have no other love left but yours—do not leave me desolate again.'

She kissed him fondly.

' My own true darling,' she answered, ' henceforth my life shall be devoted to yours. I have banished pride for ever from my heart. My only remaining pride shall be to make you regret the past as little as possible.'

' When will you come ? ' he questioned, presently.

'I am ready at any hour,' she answered, softly.

'It is not generally known to the world, as yet, that my household gods are shattered,' he said, with a rather sad smile; 'but there is no doubt the fact will be in the hands of everyone by to-morrow, your mother included. I think we had better go to-day, and let them have the enjoyment of a double scandal while they are about it. There is a train starts for Folkestone in three hours, whence we can cross to France to-night or to-morrow. Is that too short preparation for you?'

She shook her head.

'No,' she answered. 'I have nothing but myself to bring—everything can be forwarded after. I can easily get away from here, and I will meet you at the station.'

So they parted for a few hours, with that covenant made between them; and at seven o'clock the train for Folkestone carried Carn-more and Edith among its passengers.

Sad was the scene that night at her father's house, when the letter left by Edith on her dressing-table told the tale of disgrace. The proud f her and mother were humbled to the dust by the daughter's shame. In the first paroxysms of rage the marquis and his son had determined to follow the fugitive pair, but a moment's reflection told them it was useless. They might bring her back, but they could not bring back oblivion of her shame. And there they sat, far into the night—the tears of the women contrasting strangely with the stern, wordless grief of the men. It was a terrible blow to the pride of the haughty house of Allerton, which had for ages counted its men among the bravest of the brave—its women among the purest of the pure.

CHAPTER XX.

'THE AVENGER.'

IT was a delightful *bonne bouche* for the clubs the next day. Wraxall, Desmond, and several others who had been tolerably intimate with Carnmore, were discussing it, and awaiting anxiously for the appearance of Melton, who would be able, they hoped, to throw some light on the subject. Presently, to the intense relief of all, he entered.

'Thanks be to God!' exclaimed Wraxall, piously, 'he has come at last. Now, Melton, my boy, we know you are in the mystery, so make a clean breast of it at once.'

''Pon my soul,' answered Melton, seriously, 'I know as much about it as you do. I knew they were lovers once, and I suspected he had a *penchant* for her still ; but, certainly, I never expected this *esclandre.*'

Mr. Verney was the next to increase the stock of conversation.

'It is not so long ago,' he remarked, with a certain triumph in his tone, ' that Carnmore prophesied he would live to see me in the Divorce Court. It strikes me the tables are turned now : I shall, most probably, have the pleasure of seeing him. I suppose, at least, her ladyship will bring an action.'

'She or her people, no doubt,' suggested Wraxall ; ' that is, unless they wish to spite him, and prevent him from making the *amende honorable* to the fair Edith, by declining to sever his bonds.'

' The most peculiar thing about it,' remarked Mr. Verney, ' is the quiet manner in which they have carried on their little flirtation hitherto. I don't think any of us were upon the scent. I can't make it out at all satisfactorily.'

'There is nothing to make out,' replied Desmond, sharply. ' The case is clear enough : he got tired of his wife, and she got tired of having no husband ; so they made up matters together.'

'Desmond, my dear boy,' said Lord Wraxall, good-humouredly, 'you are just a little too epigrammatic for our weak intellects, and, like most brilliant people, you occasionally make great mistakes. That Lady Ardross wanted a husband, I will readily admit ; but, if that were her sole motive, why did she not take one of her own, instead of another woman's ?'

Lord Wraxall had proved himself the best dialectician of the two, and Mr. Desmond was wise enough to perceive it, and kept his own counsel. Melton was the first to break the silence that ensued.

'I regret it very much,' he said, gravely. 'I am a friend of them both ; and I think Edith Ardross was worth something better than being ostracised by the society that once did her homage.'

The depth of that remark was hardly felt by the gay worldlings to whom he spoke. Intrigues and *liaisons* are too common in the fashionable world to provoke much regret.

'It's a terrible facer for the Allertons,' said Verney, presently. 'They were never a very humble-minded family, and they thought the world of Edith.'

'Well,' said Mr. Desmond, unable to keep his caustic tongue silent any longer, 'my opinion is this—and I must beg my friend Melton's pardon if it is not very palatable to him—-I think they were both a couple of d—d fools. They could have carried on their *liaison* together very successfully without the world getting a hint of it; and I have no patience with people who let their impetuosity kick up a scandal, to the annoyance of their friends and families.' And Mr. Desmond's opinion seemed to be shared by the rest of the worldly-wise men assembled around him.

Happily, Carnmore and Edith were far removed by now from the opinions of their friends and acquaintances. They had taken rooms in one of the quietest of Parisian hotels, until they should definitely settle their future place of abode. The Rubicon once crossed, the strange country on the other side soon becomes familiar, and the first novelty of their relations to each other now soon wore off. I do not mean to say that Maud was utterly forgotten by either of them—she was remem bered remorsefully, and with shame by both ; but I am dealing with human nature as it is, and it would be idle to say that he thought more of his absent wife than his present mistress. The busy man of the world remembers keenly the days of his childhood, and perhaps sometimes sighs at the recollection of the calm, tranquil past, as contrasted with the vigorous, feverish present. But had he to deliberately choose whether he would return to the old times or remain where he was, I think there would be little doubt as to his decision.

It was on the fifth day after their arrival in Paris, that they were sitting together a short time before luncheon, when Carnmore was startled by the announcement of a visitor to see him.

No name had been sent up, merely a message delivered by a gentleman that he wished to see him on particular business.

Carnmore hesitated for a moment. He

saw the look of dismay on Edith's face, and
fancied, like her, that it must be her father or
brother come.

'Tell the gentleman,' he said, sternly, to
the waiter, 'that I can see no one unless he
furnishes me with his name.' The obsequious
attendant bowed and withdrew noiselessly,
and he turned fondly to Edith.

'Do not fear, my own darling,' he said, as
he took her in his arms and bent over her
tenderly; 'no power in this wide world shall
take you from me, now that you have given
yourself to me.'

In a few moments the waiter returned,
bearing in his hand a card. He gave it to
Carnmore, and said—

'Monsieur added that he was sure you
could not refuse to see him.'

Edith glanced at it affrightedly. She drew
an immense sigh of relief—the name on it was
Saville.

Carnmore conquered his emotion by a violent
effort, and said to the man who stood awaiting
his reply—

'Tell monsieur that I will see him immediately.'

Edith was relieved, but still puzzled. She asked, wonderingly—

'What in the world can have brought him here?'

Carnmore looked at her with a peculiar smile, and answered—

'He was an old lover of Maud's, and, I suppose, has come here to reproach me with my baseness.'

Edith paled immediately. She conjectured danger in her lover's manner.

'But what can he do?' she asked, anxiously. 'Granting that he was her old lover, and fondly attached to her, that does not give him the right to constitute himself her champion.'

'Some people take rights that no one gives them,' he said, gravely.

She rose and flung her arms passionately round his neck.

'Whenever will the consequences of my sin stop?' she cried. 'Do not see this man, Fred. He may be mad, for all you know, and may do you some violence.'

He laughed softly to himself.

'Don't alarm yourself unnecessarily, my pet,' he said, kissing her. 'I will see Mr. Saville, and I think I shall be able to hold my own, even if his love has turned his brain.' He kissed her once more, and left her with a strange presentiment of coming evil at her heart.

Saville was seated, with a fierce, restless look on his countenance, sufficiently indicative of the violent emotion under which he was labouring. He rose eagerly as Carnmore entered, and drew what seemed an immense sigh of relief to find that he had not attempted to elude him.

'I am glad to see you,' he said, quickly. 'I knew you were never a coward, and I thought you would not refuse an interview to the man whom you have wronged through *her.*'

Carnmore looked at him keenly. There was a strangeness in his manner, a rapidity in his speech and gesture, but, certainly, no evidence of insanity. His mind might have given way on one subject; but, if such tempo-

rary aberration were considered madness, no
man would be safe in getting in a passion.

'I have no wish to refuse you an interview,
Saville,' he answered, steadily; 'but it is
strange that you should come all this way to
seek me. What is your motive?'

Saville laughed bitterly, and flung his hair
back from his temples with an impatient
gesture.

'Carnmore,' he said, speaking rapidly, and
with the ring of intense feeling in his voice,
'I believe in that old world fancy of second-
sight. I think I must have had the gift
when I came to you on that day when you
wrote me of your engagement. Do you
remember what I told you then—that if Maud
Hilton was ever wronged by you, I would
constitute myself her avenger—that I would
exact the debt in full, even if it were my
own brother at whose hands I demanded
reparation? Does not your guilty conscience
tell you that the hour is come, and that I
stand here, face to face with you, her champion
to the death?'

He looked so noble as he stood there, his

handsome features lightened with his unutterable emotion, that Carnmore felt an involuntary thrill of admiration.   How superior he seemed to him at that moment—the man who, in spite of his nobleness, had failed to win the woman that the other had betrayed.

' And how shall I pay you the debt I owe ? ' he asked, in a hollow voice.

Saville's eyes shone with a fierce, thirsting light, as he answered—

' By perilling your life to mine, on equal terms, either that I may wash out her wrongs in your blood, or that you shall end the days of a most miserable and unhappy wretch.'

He ended with a half groan, as if he already had reaped alike the revenge and the oblivion he sought.

Carnmore recoiled.

' I will not fight with you,' he answered, sternly. ' Have your pure creeds and philosophies come to this, that they arm you against a fellow-Christian's life ? Can my death bring you back peace, or obliterate her wrong ? '

' No,' cried Saville, passionately : ' it is

powerless to do either, but it can give revenge—the revenge for which I have thirsted since the hour when I learned from her father's lips the story of your treachery. Do not think to escape me, Carnmore. I daresay you think me mad, but I am not; I am as sane as you are, man—sane, with a deep and deadly mission to fulfil, to the accomplishment of which the tongues of a thousand devils are urging me; stern and pitiless in the execution of a duty that is acceptable to God and man—to avenge the weak upon the strong and cruel.'

'Is it come to this,' asked Carnmore, gravely, amazed at the intense earnestness of Saville, 'that there must be murder done between two men, between whom there were the strongest ties of union?'

'Aye, it has come to this,' answered Saville, with a strange, wild laugh. 'A year ago, I would have stood by your side, and fought in your battles. To-day I thirst for your life, and am unsatisfied till I have tried to take it.'

'Your wish shall be gratified,' said Carnmore, bitterly. 'Yet, you must make some allowances for my position here. There is no one in Paris to whom I could apply to stand my second.'

'I have thought of all that,' answered Saville, impatiently. 'Tush, man! do you think I arranged my plans of revenge so ill as to let you escape, at the last moment, through a loophole like that? I saw Melton before I started, and I arranged with him that he should come over on the receipt of a telegram. Send him one now, and he will be here in the morning to meet my cousin.'

'I compliment you on the promptitude with which you have acted,' rejoined Carnmore, with a bitter sneer. 'Do not fear I will shirk my promise. Melton shall be here in the morning; and, if your hand be sufficiently steady by next day, you shall have your old friend a corpse.'

'Aye,' laughed Saville: 'your life is precious to you, I suppose, for the sake of your profligate paramour.'

Carnmore turned on him passionately.

'Silence!' he cried, fiercely, turning on him

a glance from which even Saville shrunk—a glance that told all the devil of his nature was aroused at that attack on one he loved so well. 'Revile me as you please, tack all the disgraceful epithets to my name that your hatred can invent, but spare her, unless you would wish me to cram the words down your lying throat. You have got all you wanted. I tell you, on the honour of a gentleman and a nobleman, I will give you the meeting you ask. Leave me now. Go to your own home to gloat over the prospect of your impious revenge.'

Saville did not answer. Hitherto he had had right on his side, and the other had cowered before him; but now he felt that *he* had been unmanly in attacking a woman with such a vile epithet. He drew out his card-case, and wrote his address down, and handed it to Carnmore.

He paused for a second at the door, and, turning round, advanced to Carnmore again.

'On your honour as a gentleman you promise not to fail?' he asked, with a fierce, thirsting anxiety in his eyes.

Carnmore regarded him impatiently for a second, and then replied—

'Don't let that thought disturb your sleep to-night. I have been dishonourable, and, God knows, no one feels the disgrace more keenly than I; but I am not a common swindler. I will not cheat you out of your revenge.'

He turned away, but Carnmore arrested him this time.

'One word,' he said. 'Did Maud depute you as her champion?'

'No,' he answered, fiercely. 'I learned the tale from her father. Had I seen her, I doubt not her woman's heart would have wished to spare you. Fortunately, you are in the hands of a less merciful executioner.'

Those were his last words, and, when he had finished, Carnmore sat down and wrote a telegram to Melton. It was brief, and contained these words: 'You know why I apply to you. Will you come at once?' After he had sent that off, he went back to Edith.

'Well,' she exclaimed, impatiently; 'what is the result?'

He took her in his arms, and told her all. She did not faint or cry, as weaker women would have done ; but a rigid, stony despair came over her face, as she asked, in a low voice, as half-doubting of the possibility of her request—

'You need not meet this madman?'

Carnmore smiled sadly. It seemed so bitter that there should be this uncertainty in enjoying his beautiful prize.

'Edith, darling,' he said, tenderly, 'would you have the world say your lover proved himself a coward, and dared not face the champion of the woman he had wronged? Such was never the wish of the women of your house. They were the first to buckle on the armour of their sons and husbands when honour demanded that they should peril their lives. I have done a great and deadly wrong for your sweet sake. My life is the only reparation I can offer. You would not have me so contemptible as to refuse to stake it against *his*?'

Edith bowed her head in mute despair upon his breast.

'Oh, my own darling,' she sobbed, bitterly, 'the hand that kills you will slay me too: they will have to lay us both in the same grave!'

CHAPTER XXI.

'DEATH THE ARBITRATOR.'

MELTON arrived the next morning. He
possessed a more than ordinary fashionable
laxity in morals, and he was not, therefore,
a man to turn the cold shoulder to his friend,
because he had run away from his wife, particularly when he was scarcely in receipt of
any authentic information as to who was the
most culpable party. The truth had begun
to leak out a little. It had got generally
whispered abroad that Lady Carnmore had
left her husband's home on the day of the
Duchess of Featherstone's *fête*, and the day on
which Carnmore and Edith went away was
known for a certainty. It was, of course,
surmised from these facts that the real cause

of separation must have occurred in the grounds of the duchess, but mere guesses, after all, are very unsatisfactory things. So, as usual in such cases, both the women came in for a considerable share of blame : Maud being thought by many to have been guilty of precipitancy in so suddenly asserting her independence ; while Edith, of course, received unqualified condemnation at the hands of everybody. With regard to Carnmore's share in the business, the female members of the Areopagus, which sat solemnly on the case, could return no satisfactory verdict. With the leniency characteristic of women in judging between their own and the other sex, they were rather inclined to look upon him as the victim of circumstances, and to pour all the vials of their wrath upon the devoted heads of the two women with whom he was connected.

Edith and Carnmore were sitting together as Melton entered. He shook hands with his friend first, and then advanced to her. His presence there that morning seemed like a message from the past, and awoke keenly in her the sense of the shame which her few days' happiness, and this last day's grief, had seemed almost to ·obliterate. She held out her hand with an averted face, and, in a tearful voice, asked—

'Oh, Ernest, what have they said of me at home?'

Melton looked very embarrassed, and paused, searching in his own mind for some suitable reply; but, before he could answer, Carnmore stepped to her side, and, putting his arm round her waist, fondly said—

'How can it matter what the world has said, my darling? We have taken our hearts and loves into our own hands. Henceforth, the babble of those we left behind can never disturb us.'

She lifted up her tear-stained face to his penitently.

'Forgive me, Fred, dearest, for my selfishness in thinking of that now,' she said, in a low voice: 'I only regret the past for your sake, to think that it has placed you in peril.'

Melton turned away, visibly affected. He was not a man of very deep feeling, perhaps— no great sorrows or joys had disturbed the

calm, every-day brightness of his life ; but I
think he felt, at that moment, that there was
a love between these two beyond the ordinary
comprehension of the world.

'I am deeply grateful to you for your
promptitude in answering my request, Melton,'
said Carnmore, presently. ' If you will come
with me for a few minutes, we will discuss
this painful business.'

He preceded him into another room, and,
when they were seated, said—

' You have seen this incomprehensible madman ? '

' Yes ; he called on me the day he started
for here, and told me he was going over with
his cousin, Harry Saville, for the purpose of
calling you out.   I tried to reason with him
to the best of my ability—urged that duelling,
in the present day, was utterly absurd, and
that you would be fully justified in refusing
to meet him.   My arguments were of no avail
whatever.   He contended that there was only
one way of reparation, and that, unless you
were a poltroon, you would accede to it.   I
suppose you intend to do so ? '

'I am afraid I must,' answered Carnmore, seriously. 'I am no coward, and I do not dread to meet his pistol; but, for that poor girl's sake, I would have willingly avoided it, had it lain in my power. But I feel, Melton, what he says, that it is the only reparation which I can offer for the deep and deadly wrong I have done her.'

'So be it, then,' answered Melton. 'Were I in your place, I think I should feel bound to do the same. I will go and see Harry Saville at once.'

So saying, he left the hotel, and took a carriage to where Saville was staying. He knew his cousin well—a rather poverty-stricken lieutenant in the 2nd 'Life,' who managed to keep his head above water in a most miraculous manner, considering the brevity of the supplies from home.

'This is a most extraordinary affair,' said Melton, after they had saluted. The guardsman shrugged his shoulders. His general demeanour did not argue much capacity for emotion, and he utterly failed to comprehend how another woman's wrong could drive a man beside himself.

'You are right,' he said, carelessly. 'I
don't pretend to understand it myself; but he
asked me to act for him, and, of course, I
could not decently refuse. How does Lady
Ardross enjoy the prospect of her lover's
facing his old friend—that is to say, if she
has heard of it? Perhaps he has not told
her?'

. 'Yes, she knows it ; there was no help for
it, I believe. She knew Saville called on him,
and he was not diplomatic enough to invent
any reason for his unexpected appearance.
She bears herself pretty bravely ; but, I think,
if anything serious comes of to-morrow, she
will get her death-blow.'

The lieutenant was naturally curious, and
asked a good many more questions; but Melton
tried to elude them as much as possible, for
he knew his companion would only be too
delighted to give a 'true and correct' account
of the scandal when he returned to town.
Besides, he was not in possession of much
information himself, for Carnmore had not, as
yet, confided to him the story of his separation
from Maud.

They soon arranged their deadly business.
The place of meeting was the Bois de Boulogne,
the time six o'clock. As Melton rose to go
the young guardsman said, with more heartiness than had hitherto been apparent in his
tone or manner—

'I think we have got everything settled
satisfactorily now. You say you know a
surgeon you can procure to be on the ground,
in case such services are required? I only
hope the shots will miss, and that we can
take them away without bloodshed, and with
honour.'

It was a miserable night for Edith. Carnmore soon slept soundly; but she lay in his
arms with scarcely a few minutes' respite from
the hideous thought of the morning's work.
He rose at five, and she with him; and they
descended to the room, where they found
Melton awaiting them, with the slight break-
fast that he had ordered over night. It wanted
twenty minutes to six as they entered, and
Edith turned deadly pale as she remembered
that in ten minutes more she might take her
last farewell of him.

Melton rose up, and went over to her, taking her hand in his own.

'You must not imagine the worst while we are gone,' he said, cheerfully. 'Saville is no shot, his cousin tells me; and even if he were, the chances are that his present excitement goes far to preclude the probability of his hand being sufficiently steady to achieve anything deadly. Carnmore intends to fire in the air, and I think it most likely that you will see us back safe and sound, with our honour perfectly satisfied.'

Edith tried to summon a faint smile, but in vain. She sank down into the nearest chair, and buried her face in her handkerchief, sobbing quietly and bitterly. Melton wisely left the room. It was better that that solemn farewell should be taken in secret.

In ten minutes Carnmore joined his friend. That parting had unnerved him terribly; but by the time they arrived on the ground he had recovered his usual self-possession. Saville and his cousin, with the surgeon, were there awaiting them, and the first of the three was pacing up and down restlessly, as if impatient of even the necessary delay that must elapse ere he could take his revenge.

The distance was measured, and the pistols put into their hands. Melton was to give the word. He did so slowly; and, as the 'three' was uttered, the report of one pistol rang out in the stillness. The next instant Carnmore fired his in the air.

Saville's shot had missed; but, to the surprise of everyone, he staggered and fell as Carnmore fired his pistol. They ran to him, and the surgeon hastily put his hand over his heart. He was quite dead. He had escaped death at the hands of his old friend, only to meet it through the violence of his own conflicting emotions.

Carnmore gazed sorrowfully on the man whose hand had so often clasped his in friendship, and which the madness of his unhappy love had at last armed against his life.

'Thank God,' he muttered fervently to himself, 'he is not stained with murder.'

CHAPTER XXII.

'FADING AWAY.'

Two years had elapsed since that memorable day on which the Duchess of Featherstone gave her *fête*. Maud had obtained a divorce, and Edith had been married to her lover too late to save her fair fame. They had lived abroad all the time, devoting their lives to each other, and finding, in their mutual love, a compensation for the gay world whose sense of propriety they had outraged. Yet they were happy in their new existence; and, had it not been for that deep, abiding remorse for the peace they had shattered, there was nothing to regret on either side.

But there is no immunity for happiness that is built upon others' misery. Sooner or later the steps of the inexorable Nemesis steal on the guilty, and avenge insulted justice. The chains in which they had bound their love were soon to be shattered by a strong and ruthless hand. There was another who panted and thirsted to feed on her beauty as fiercely as her lover had done—who longed to lay his blasting kiss upon her perfect lips, to quench the fire in those wondrous eyes. That other was the grim conqueror—Death. Already was his shadowy embrace around her, fighting desperately with the mortal clasp that shuddered to let her go.

Edith had never been strong, and I doubt not that she might have sown the seeds of consumption in the hothouse atmosphere of the fashionable saloons in which she had passed her life. But I think shame and remorse, both of which tell more heavily on a woman than a man, had done their work upon her fragile frame. It was not only the remorse for her own wrong-doing that was gnawing so fiercely at her heart, but the thought that her selfish love had wrecked her husband's life. She had never borne the shadow of a reproach from him on this account.

He was gentleness itself to the woman for whom he had renounced all; but none the less did she feel convinced, in her own mind, that he must regret the step by which he had exiled himself from every ambition of existence.

And Carnmore gazed on her day after day, and noted the deepening of that hectic flush, which only seemed to make her more beautiful for the grave, the painful brilliancy of those dark eyes, the wasting of the form; and an awful pain smote his heart. Two years of happiness—two little, short years—and was his beautiful love to be taken from him like this! Had he won her at last, only to yield her to the cold embrace of Death! Night after night did he pray, with a fervency that his awful dread alone taught him, that, if possible, this bitter cup might not be proffered to his lips.

It was hard for him to part with her thus; he had thrown away every other chance of happiness, and centred all in her. When she was taken from him, what was there left in life? Life without love is a blank; but life out of which love has gone for ever is but a living-death. There was the wide world left, it is true ; ambition and talent could still be his ; but what recked he of such, when the one for whom he had sacrificed these in the past should be lying in her grave.

And it smote Edith's heart cruelly to think she must leave him alone so soon. Had it lain in her own power to arrest her fatal disease, it is needless to say no self-sacrifice would have been wanting ; but the remorse and shame of the first year had done their work too effectually. The doctors could give her no hope ; care and attention might do something to prolong her life, they said ; but to save it was not in their hands. She was ordered from one place to another ; Carnmore hoping almost against hope that she might yet be spared. But time wore on, and deeper grew the flush on her cheek—more painfully brilliant the light of her dark eyes. He felt that the end was very near.

They were at Cânnes : she had been recommended there as a last resource. All that love and devotion could do for her was done, but in vain. He sat by her side all day, never leaving her for a moment; and he knew that he must not lose any of those precious hours, for they were getting numbered.

She was one day reclining on the couch, to which of late she had become a frequent prisoner. He was in an easy chair beside her, and her cheek was pillowed against his. Presently she said—

'We have been very happy, dearest, have we not?'

He folded his arms closelier around her—she was fast slipping from that embrace now— as he answered—

'I could scarcely have dreamed of greater happiness.'

'And very soon,' she said, mournfully, 'you will have to look upon our love as all a dream; will you not?'

'Oh, Edith, my own darling,' he cried, with a sharp pain in his voice—it seemed so fearful to gaze into the utter blankness that would be when she left—'do not talk of that yet. There is hope even at the eleventh hour.'

She smiled sadly. 'My love is selfish to the last, Fred,' she said, with a faint smile.

'I would like to take you with me to where I am going.'

'No need to wish that,' he answered, earnestly. 'I shall soon follow you of my own accord. If prayers can woo death, it will not be long before we are lying side by side in the same grave.'

She looked up at him with a bright smile.

'It makes me so happy to think I have been so dear to you,' she said. 'Sometimes when you have looked sad and gloomy, I fancied that you were regretting our love.'

'Never, my own darling.' he answered, straining her passionately to his breast. 'I have sometimes, nay always, felt remorseful when I have thought of *her* ; but I have never wished to undo the past, save on her account.'

'Would you have ordered your destiny otherwise could you have had the choice of loving me or not?' she asked, timidly.

'Oh, Edith, dearest,' he said, earnestly, 'it is but right I should say yes, but how can I palter with the truth ? Has not my love for you been the one bright thing of my life? How could I have chosen a life from which

that brightness should be exiled? Yes, I
would live my past again sooner than a new
existence in which no thought of you should
share. The rapture of our early loves—the
agony of our separation—the doubt of our
second meeting—aye, even the wrong done to
her who loved me so truly—I would live them
all over again for the same reward that I have
reaped now, to call you wholly and solely
mine; no matter what the penalty I called
down upon my own head. I have had you
two years to myself, and for all former or after
years of misery I have been amply compen-
sated.'

'My own darling,' she murmured, softly, as
she pillowed her wan and burning cheek
against his, 'how I can repent, too late, the
folly that has shipwrecked our lives. To
think that one little word of mine could have
given us that happiness which we have had to
reap from others' misery. Oh, how I shudder
at the thought of dying with all this weight
of guilt upon my soul.'

He kissed her passionately. 'The tempter,
not the tempted, is the most to blame,' he

said, soothingly. 'It was I who wooed you to wrong-doing. Trust me, darling, that will be remembered by a merciful Judge.'

'Nay,' she cried, earnestly, 'you shall not take all the burden upon yourself. It was my fatal beauty that lured you to madness. It seems such a mockery now to talk of beauty, as if these poor pallid features, in which I once took such pride, could have any influence now; but they were your bane, were they not, my own dearest?'

'It was fate that crossed the threads of our lives,' he said, with a mournful smile. 'Our hearts were drawn together as the magnet towards the pole. The only folly was when we attempted to sunder them.'

She was silent for some time. That slight exertion of talking had exhausted her; but presently she said—

'When the last comes, dearest, I should like to see my family again, and ask their forgiveness. Do you think they would come?'

'I should scarcely think they would refuse,' he answered, bitterly. 'You have outraged their pride, but your life will pay the penalty You can scarcely make a greater reparation.'

She seemed satisfied with that answer, and dozed off to sleep presently. He held her tenderly in his arms, and thought with shuddering of the end that was so near. His eyes filled with blinding tears as he looked on the fair face, so beautiful still, in spite of the fatal signs of death.

'God grant,' he said, fervently, as he bent over her, and pressed his lips passionately to hers, 'that I may follow her quickly.'

CHAPTER XXIII.

'AT PEACE.'

THE last had come. Edith was face to face with death, and Carnmore had written to her mother, summoning her to her bedside.

The Marquis of Allerton, his wife, and Florence came immediately on the receipt of that letter. The Earl of Carrick, her only brother left in England—the other two were in India—had been telegraphed for to Scotland; but he must, at least, be a day behind the others.

No communication had passed between them since they had left England; and at a less solemn time Carnmore would have felt some shame at meeting those whom he had injured so cruelly through their daughter; but he scarcely felt this now. He advanced to meet them with outstretched hand.

'Lord Allerton,' he said, gravely, 'I know you have to complain of deep wrong at my hands, but this is scarcely a fitting time for resentment. Edith's life will pay the penalty of her sin; and, I think, you would forgive me, too, could you read my broken heart. Let us, at least, preserve the semblance of peace. Do not let us harrow her deathbed by our inconsiderate anger.'

The marchioness and Florence, both women-like, took the hand that was extended to them; but the father could not forget his pride and resentment so far as that.

'Do you think that I can crush a father's love out of my heart easily?' he said, hoarsely. 'But, how can I forget, that had it not been for you, my child could have been honoured as well as loved?'

Carnmore turned away sadly, and led the way to Edith's room. She uttered a great cry of joy as she saw them enter, and flung her arms around them in succession with passionate fervour. Her husband thought it

best to leave them together for a while, and
was about to leave the room, but Edith
stopped him instantly.

'Do not go away, Fred,' she said, pleadingly;
'you will not have me long with you. Besides,
I want to ask if they will forgive us both?'

She turned eagerly to the mournful faces
that were watching her own, and read in them
pardon for her sin; but that was not all she
wanted.

'Have you forgiven him, too?' she asked,
softly.

Her mother answered gently, 'Yes.' But
the marquis could not become such a good
Christian as that yet. She read his hesitation, and turned to him beseechingly.

'Oh, father, dearest!' she said, earnestly,
'I was the most to blame, indeed I was. If
you have pardoned me, you cannot refuse
to forgive him. For your dying daughter's
sake, say you do. Do not embitter my last
moments thus. Let there be no division
amongst those with whom I wish to be at
peace.'

He could not resist that appeal. He rose,

with the tears in his eyes, and held out his hand to his son-in-law. 'You have my forgiveness,' he said, 'if it will make her happier.'

'And now I am contented,' she said, softly; 'at least, as contented as I can be. Life has been brighter for me in one great thing these last two years than ever it had been before, and I would fain have lived a little longer; but God's will be done.'

There was no sound in the room save that of the stifled sobbing of her mother and Florence. Strange to say, the grief around her seemed to have the effect of rendering her calmer.

'Do not weep, mother dearest, and you, Florence darling, who were always so kind to me. Many a night have I lain awake, thinking of the grief and shame I must have brought upon your happy faces; but you will forgive me now, will you not? You knew how wilful and proud I was even as a little child, and had it not been for these I could have been a happy woman, loved and loving; but I sacrificed my life to my pride, while I was yet too heedless and inexperienced to count the cost.

You do not know how madly we loved each other, or else I think you would find excuse for us even now. I fought so long against my own heart, I preserved so steadfastly my loyalty to my husband, although my guilty love was consuming me all the time; and then, when he died, I seemed to lose my power of self-control—I let my love appear too plainly, till it awoke a mutual madness in him; and, so, one day our secret was discovered by his wife, and she left him, as, indeed, she had a right in doing; and, after that, could I refuse to reward him for all he had suffered and lost for my sake?'

Her hand stole tenderly to his as she said this, and she looked up at him with those great dark eyes, from which death could not banish the deep, intense passion. It seemed such a sweet task to try and exculpate him from all blame in the eyes of others. Her mother and Florence knew at that hour, if they had never guessed it before, that there was a love between these two far beyond ordinary comprehension.

For three more weary days did Edith battle

bravely with her grim foe. I think it must have been only her intense love that kept her alive. She had scarcely seemed to recognise the full agony of separation until the time drew so near, and then she would have given worlds to take him with her.

On the fourth day, however, she yielded, and her ghastly vanquisher held her firmly in his grasp. He had spared her beauty till the last—that fair, proud beauty, which had been her undoing. Wan and emaciated as she was, she looked still lovely in the eyes from whose gaze she was fast vanishing.

About an hour before she died she beckoned her husband to her side, and nestled herself in his arms.

'Fold them closely round me, my own darling,' she whispered, softly ; 'they are my fitting resting-place. Do you forgive me for all my past folly ?'

He bent over her, and pressed his quivering lips to hers. In spite of the nearness of death, there was passion still in the kiss that she gave him. To the last, love was stronger than all.

They watched her, tearfully and mournfully, as she dozed off into a deathlike sleep. For an hour she lay like that; and then, suddenly, she awoke with a shiver, and clasped her husband with all her dying strength. He bent over her again, and she struggled convulsively to lift her lip to his. She just brushed them, and then fell back. Her life had expired in that last passionate caress.

There she lay on the pillow, cold and dead; her husband's tears raining down on her lifeless face, her husband's kisses showering down on her mute lips, fatally fair for her own and others' peace no longer. If suffering could atone for sin, she had paid her penalty; and in the world to where she has gone, I think the remorse which cost her life will have some weight with that merciful Judge, whose sentence on the repentant sinner was to 'go and sin no more.'

CHAPTER XXIV.

'FORGIVEN.'

It is in the height of the season. A group of club loungers are discussing some recent news, apparently with great interest.

'Not a year since she died,' says Lord Wraxall, sympathetically. 'Poor fellow! how he must have loved her.'

'Melton told me the particulars of his death this morning,' says Lord Glengariff. 'His man went into his room, as usual, to call him, and found him dead in his bed, lying quite calmly and peacefully.'

'Extraordinary death!' remarks Desmond. 'Heart disease, probably.'

'Broken heart, more likely,' answers Wraxall. 'There can be such a thing, although, I daresay, you don't believe it, Desmond.

Poor Carnmore. A sad ending for one who would have made such a mark in the world but for that unhappy affair with Lady Ardross.'

The scandal had been well-nigh forgotten by now, but the sudden news of Carnmore's death revived it for a bit. It reached Maud Hilton in that quiet retreat among the Devonshire hills which she had made in greater part her home before the letter which he had ordered to be forwarded on his death, came to her hands.

The sight of that well-known handwriting caused a strange pain at Maud's heart. Her love for him had been the one bright dream of her life. She had been awakened from it rudely, but she could not forget it had ever been.

It was a short but earnest letter. It affirmed the sincerity of his love when he wooed her, and the remorse he had felt for his wrong, and concluded with asking her forgiveness.

It was a hot summer's afternoon at the end of August that a stately and beautiful woman, yet on whose beauty there seemed to hover the shadow of a great sorrow, stood by the grave which held Carnmore and Edith.

Her tears dropped fast as she thought of the early time when the dead man's love had been all to her, ere yet she had learned to know his heart was another's.

'Poor fellow!' she murmured, sadly, 'he has paid a heavy penalty for his wrong. Yet, I suppose, in marrying me he only did what many would have done. I believe he would have kept faithful had I not discovered his secret. After all, she loved him first; and to love him once was, I fear, to love him for ever. Their hearts were one in life, and in death they are still united. It was I who came between them.'

And, so, over her dead husband's grave did Maud find excuse for his sin; and I think that when sleep, long wooed in vain, came to her eyes that night, he was forgiven freely by the woman he had wronged so cruelly.

THE END.

John Heywood, Excelsior Printing Works, Hulme Hall Road, Manchester.

[MARCH, 1873.

SAMUEL TINSLEY'S

NEW

PUBLICATIONS.

LONDON:

SAMUEL TINSLEY, Publisher,

10, SOUTHAMPTON STREET, STRAND, W.C.

. *Totally distinct from any other firm of Publishers.*

SAMUEL TINSLEY'S
NEW PUBLICATIONS.

THE POPULAR NEW NOVELS, AT ALL LIBRARIES IN TOWN AND COUNTRY.

ALDEN OF ALDENHOLME. By GEORGE SMITH. 3 Vols., 31s. 6d.

"Pure and graceful. . . . . Above the average."—*Athenæum*
"The moral tendencies of the book are excellent."—*Globe.*
"The idea of the book is well conceived, and the lesson it is intended to teach eminently sound and wholesome."—*Graphic.*
"A highly interesting and well-conceived story, and the plot is not only cleverly constructed, but it is also unfolded in a skilful and natural manner."—*Echo.*

THE BARONET'S CROSS. By MARY MEEKE, Author of "Marion's Path through Shadow and Sunshine." 2 vols., 21s.

BETWEEN TWO LOVES. By ROBERT J. GRIFFITHS, LL.D. 3 vols., 31s. 6d.

"A tolerably substantial tale, seasoned with a fair allowance of love and villainy . . . . . . It is written in a good plain style."—*Illustrated London News.*

BUILDING UPON SAND. By ELIZABETH J. LYSAGHT. Crown 8vo, 10s. 6d.

"It is an eminently lady-like story, and pleasantly told. . We can safely recommend 'Building upon Sand.'"—*Graphic.*

THE D'EYNCOURTS OF FAIRLEIGH. By THOMAS ROWLAND SKEMP. 3 vols., 31s. 6d.

"A stirring and vigorous novel."—*Court Circular.*
"Written in a light, lively style; full of stirring adventures by land and sea."—*Echo.*
"An exceedingly readable novel, full of various and sustained interest. . . . . The interest is well kept up all through."—*Daily Telegraph.*

FAIR, BUT NOT WISE. By Mrs. FORREST GRANT. 2 vols., 21s.

"'Fair, but not Wise' possesses considerable merit, and is both cleverly and powerfully written. If earnest, it is yet amusing and sometimes humorous, and the interest is well sustained from the first to the last page."—*Court Express.*

Samuel Tinsley, 10, Southampton Street, Strand.

A DESPERATE CHARACTER:

A TALE OF THE GOLD FEVER.

BY W. THOMSON-GREGG.

3 vols., 31s. 6d.

"The story is very interesting ; it is written in a light, pleasing style, and the descriptions of life and scenery in the Antipodes are graphic and well done."—*Echo.*

"Hubert de Burgh's experiences at the gold-fields and elsewhere are all told very well and cleverly. . . . His conversion is one of the most remarkable things that has ever been written of anywhere."—*Scotsman.*

"A novel which cannot fail to interest. It describes the wild life of the Australian gold-fields with a picturesqueness of style and quickness of observation which render the story very attractive, while the new and unbroken ground traversed is capable of yielding a rich harvest of fiction. . . . . The author has a considerable facility with his pen ; his places and people form themselves clearly before the reader, whom he transports, as with the famous carpet of the Arabian story-teller, to other shores in the twinkling of an eye."—*Daily News.*

"Mr. Thomson-Gregg gives us an exceedingly interesting insight into Australian life. . . . The tale of De Burgh's adventures, his courtship and conversion, and subsequent marriage to Clara, is told in a masterly manner. . . . . . On the whole, the work is full of pleasant incidents, and is singularly free from anything which can give offence to the most sensitive mind. At the same time a rich vein of humour is apparent throughout, and the liveliness of the tale is never allowed to flag."—*Daily Telegraph.*

"Mr. Thomson-Gregg has succeeded in depicting the toils and gains of gold-digging, squatting, and manual labour, with a vigour and faithfulness which cannot fail to please those Australian critics who have hitherto complained that no writer has been able to convey any idea of the strenuous exertion, the keen excitement, and the brilliant successes which make the life of a colonist so attractive. He has painted for us a series of pictures of the lovely luxuriant vegetation, the sudden changes of climate, the mixed nationalities, and the restless struggle for wealth, which are all so typical of the country which its adopted children fondly term the land of promise. He has shown us Australian life from many points of view. . . . . George and Charles Woodward were unfit for the stern exigencies of colonial life. The touches by which their weakness and their desponding fears are rendered are very delicate and powerful. Their pettish despair, languid fatigues, and frequent blushes ; the bitter tears that fill their eyes when they feel shame or grief, their mutual jealousy, and the susceptibility which causes them both to fall wildly in love with the doctor's pretty daughter, are all described with a quiet power which makes them stand out with distinct individuality. . . . . There is true pathos in the scene where Charley finds his brother dying in the hospital, where he had been too proud to give his own name, and where these gentle unfortunate companions kiss and part for the last time ; and in Charley's bitter cry, 'My brother, my brother ! oh, I wish I was with you, for your troubles are over and mine are but begun.' The artistic skill with which Mr. Thomson-Gregg has worked out all his characters, but especially these brothers, would make his book remarkable, independently of the additional interest it derives from its faithful, spirited pictures of life under the Southern Cross, and the terse condensed humour of the conversations. There is a jovial gaiety about the book from beginning to end that is essentially colonial, and it will be welcomed in the many homes whence some son or brother has gone to engage in the struggle for wealth in the busy Australian Colonies it so well describes, as well as by all who can appreciate the well-told tale of a hard-fought fight."—*Morning Post.*

Samuel Tinsley, 10, Southampton Street, Strand.

FIRST AND LAST. By F. Vernon-White. 2 vols., 21s.

GOLDEN MEMORIES. By Effie Leigh. 2 vols., 21s

GRAYWORTH: a Story of Country Life. By Carey Hazlewood. 3 vols., 31s. 6d.

" Carey Hazlewood has a keen eye for character, and can write well. The contrast between the practical and the ideal life, as exemplified in the characters of Dr. Perry and Mr. Benson, the over-conscientious curate, is admirably drawn."—*Examiner.*

"Many traces of good feeling and good taste, little touches of quiet humour, denoting kindly observation, and a genuine love of the country."—*Standard.*

" There is something idylic in the chapter in which Abel Armstrong's wooing is described, and nothing could be prettier than the way in which Miss Mary Anna Brown contrives to let the simple-minded curate understand that she loves him, and that unless he returns her love she must die."—*Athenæum.*

NO FATHERLAND. By Madame Von Oppen. 2 vols., 21s.

PERCY LOCKHART. By F. W. Baxter. 2 vols., 21s.

" A bright, fresh, healthy story. . . . . The book is eminently readable. . . . Some readers will perhaps wish that it filled three volumes instead of two. It is not often that we see ground for echoing such a wish, but in the present instance it is both just and natural to do so."—*Standard.*

"Mr. Frank Baxter, unfortunately some time deceased, was a member of the locally-influential and much-respected family in Dundee of that name, and devoted himself in the intervals of business to literary pursuits. As an interesting work of fiction, fresh, breezy, and healthful in style and moral, we heartily commend 'Percy Lockhart.'"—*Edinburgh Courant.*

" After the perfumed atmosphere of many recent novels, it is really refreshing to get a breath of mountain air. The author writes like a gentleman."—*Athenæum.*

"The novel altogether deserves praise. It is healthy in tone, interesting in plot and incident, and generally so well written that few persons would be able justly to find fault with it."—*Scotsman.*

" Few better novels in these days find their way into circulating libraries, and we cannot doubt its success. If a story which holds the reader, though it has no dash of sensationalism—if graphic portraitures of character, and lively, thoughtful, and instructive colloquies, and animated and accurate descriptions of varied scenery, entitle a work of fiction to favourable reception—this one has a good claim."—*Dundee Courier.*

RAVENSDALE. 3 vols., 31s. 6d.

"A well-told, natural, and wholesome story."—*Standard*.

"This powerfully-written tale is founded on facts connected with that unsettled period of Irish history which succeeded the Rebellion of 1798. . . . . . The interest of a well-managed and very complicated plot is sustained to the end; and the fresh, healthy tone of the book, as well as the command of language possessed by its author in such a remarkable degree, will insure for it a wide popularity, as it contrasts strongly with the vapid and sentimental, as well as with the sensational publications so rife at the present day."—*Morning Post*.

"The story gives us a tolerable idea of Ireland just after the Union, and is singularly free from exaggeration of every sort. The unsettled state of society at that time is brought clearly before us. After the lapse of two generations there is no impropriety in bringing on to the scene some of the actors in the exciting drama which took place at the close of the last century; and life is given to the story by the introduction of many of those who played at that time prominent parts in Irish history. . . . . It is fairly interesting, and thoroughly wholesome in tone."—*Athenæum*.

"No one can deny merit to the new writer of this romance. . . . To write of the Gaelic people, who are, perhaps, inconveniently asserting themselves all over the world, in the style that was popular thirty years ago, would be too flagrant an anachronism. Notions of the Irish are yearly more and more confused; and opinions concerning their merits and prospects are in so transitional a state that, except, perhaps, in some Irish circles, old estimates are generally dismissed as obsolete. Let us praise the author of 'Ravensdale' for perceiving this. His peasants are not 'men whose heads do grow beneath their shoulders.' He avoids the *patois*, so rankly racy of the soil, which has been generally used in Irish fiction; nor does he indulge in the conventional 'local colour' so wonderful in height and depth that there is nothing like it in other human societies. . . . It is free from vulgarity and immorality, from tricks of style and imitation of those dealers in Irish fiction who, from Fynes Moryson to the author of 'Realities of Irish Life,' have done irreparable mischief by using the arts of caricature, and every method of insincerity, to increase the antagonism between English and Irish modes of life, and impede that mutual acquaintance which might have secured mutual respect."—*Saturday Review*.

THE SEDGEBOROUGH WORLD. By A. FAREBROTHER. 2 vols., 21s.

"There is much cleverness in this novel. . . . There is certainly promise in the author."—*Graphic*.

"There is no little novelty and a large fund of amusement in 'The Sedgeborough World.'"—*Illustrated London News*.

SONS OF DIVES. 2 vols., 21s.

"The novel has merit, and is very readable."—*Echo*.

"A well-principled and natural story."—*Athenæum*.

"A fair, readable, business-like, well-ending love story. . . . . The volumes bear no author's name, but that does not interfere with the interest of them."—*Illustrated London News*.

"A good and well told story of modern life, with characters that interest and a plot that stimulates. . . . . The novel is to be commended; and readers in search of amusement will do well to place its name in their lists."—*Sunday Times*.

"The reader is not taken into scenes of poverty or wretchedness, but kept in rich drawing-rooms and well-appointed country houses, while every character in whom any interest can be taken reaches the height of good fortune and happiness before leaving the stage."—*Globe*.

"A pleasant and readable little story. . . . . . The incidents are natural, and the plot, though slight, is well contrived and well worked out, so that they may be fairly left to the reader's own quiet investigation and judgment."—*Standard*.

THE SURGEON'S SECRET. By Sydney Mostyn. Crown 8vo, 10s. 6d.

"A most exciting novel—the best on our list. It may be fairly recommended as a very extraordinary book."—*John Bull.*

"A stirring drama, with a number of closely-connected scenes, in which there are not a few legitimately sensational situations. There are many spirited passages."—*Public Opinion.*

THE TRUE STORY OF HUGH NOBLE'S FLIGHT. By the Authoress of "What Her Face Said." 10s. 6d.

"A pleasant story, with touches of exquisite pathos, well told by one who is master of an excellent and sprightly style."—*Standard.*

" An unpretending, yet very pathetic story. . . . We can congratulate the author on having achieved a signal success."—*Graphic.*

"The observation of men and women, the insight into motives, the analysis of what is called character, all these show that half a century's experience has not been thrown away on the writer, and through her may suggest much that will be appreciated by her readers."—*Athenæum.*

WAGES : a Story in Three Books. 3 vols., 31s. 6d.

WEIMAR'S TRUST. By Mrs. Edward Christian. 3 vols., 31s. 6d.

WILL SHE BEAR IT ? A Tale of the Weald. 3 vols., 31s. 6d.

" This is a clever story, easily and naturally told, and the reader's interest sustained throughout. . . . . A pleasant, readable book, such as we can heartily recommend as likely to do good service in the dull and foggy days before us."—*Spectator.*

"Written with simplicity, good feeling, and good sense, and marked throughout by a high moral tone, which is all the more powerful from never being obtrusive. . . . . The interest is kept up with increasing power to the last."—*Standard.*

" The story is a love tale, and the interest is almost entirely confined to the heroine, who is certainly a good girl, bearing unmerited sorrow with patience and resignation. The heroine's young friend is also attractive. . . . As for the seventh commandment, its breach is not even alluded to."—*Athenæum.*

" There is abundance of individuality in the story, the characters are all genuine, and the atmosphere of the novel is agreeable. It is really interesting. On the whole, it may be recommended for general perusal."—*Sunday Times.*

" A story of English country life in the early part of this century, thoroughly clever and interesting, and pleasantly and naturally told. . . . . . . In every way we entertain a very high opinion of this book."—*Graphic.*

Samuel Tinsley, 10, Southampton Street, Strand.

NOTICE.—TO PROMOTERS OF THE TEMPERANCE CAUSE, ETC.

THE INSIDIOUS THIEF:

A TALE FOR HUMBLE FOLKS.

BY ONE OF THEMSELVES.

Crown 8vo, 5s. Second Edition.

"Ought to be in the hands of every temperance lecturer and missionary in the kingdom, and in every Mechanics' Institute library, for it is an able, interesting, and persuasive volume on the evils of strong drink, that cannot fail to do much good."—*Court Circular*.

"Have we here a new writer or a practised hand turned to a new subject? In either case we congratulate ourselves upon our good fortune. We do not hesitate to characterise 'The Insidious Thief' as a most original and powerful book. . . . . The only disappointment felt on concluding the perusal of the last chapter was that a story so humorous and pathetic, so powerful and absorbing, had come to an end."—*The Templar*.

"Few will take it up without going right through it with avidity, and without being converted to teetotalism—feeling a deeper hatred to that frightful and damnable vice which works such terrible results. . . . Our temperance readers ought to get this book and lend it to all their friends."—*Literary World*.

"The power with which this story is wrought out is very remarkable, and its pages literally sparkle with home truths and loving sympathies. From the first chapter to the last the interest of the reader is unflaggingly sustained. The characters are full of life, energy, and reality. We take to our hearts, as it were, the eccentric old sailor, Uncle Wood. . . . . We heartily recommend 'The Insidious Thief' to all who wish to do battle with the iniquitous and evil-propagating drinking customs of our age. It will arm them with many a keen and trenchant weapon for the battle that must be fought."—*English Good Templar*.

"'The Insidious Thief' is a protest against the prevalent abuse of strong drinks. We see on the title page that it is a 'Tale for Humble Folks, written by One of Themselves;' and, we think, the simple earnestness of the style will bring its advice home to its readers among the lower classes. The author does not fall into the common error of condemning every man who drinks a glass of beer—that wholesale condemnation does a great deal more harm than good. There are some humorous touches in it, and the character of Uncle Wood, the sailor, is excellently drawn. . . . We recommend this volume warmly to our readers. It is excellently printed and elegantly bound."—*Lloyd's Weekly Newspaper*.

"We are bound to say that it is in some respects very powerful, and in no sense the 'ordinary temperance tale'—if by that is meant a hash of weak and unnaturally overdrawn portraits and long inconsequent sermonisings. This story is carefully written, and clearly by a practised hand, who knows low life well, both in its worst and best aspects, and who can artistically select and condense, and thus gain forcible dramatic effects, not unrelieved occasionally by a self-controlled humour, which would be sardonic now and then, were it not that it is purified by the unmistakable presence of a certain patient wisdom which waits for results. Here and there this writer, when dealing with certain types, reminds us, in his recurring sudden quaintness of touch, of Mr. Henry Holbeach ; and again, in his power of deepening an impression by a subtle representation of detail, of Mr. Farjeon. . . . . A book of this sort should be tested by the whole impression produced ; and in this respect it stands the test well—better than any other temperance story we remember to have read. It is, in truth, valuable also for practical hints ; and, in the best form, sets forth lessons which most of us would be better to remember, with regard to adverse influences at work among the struggling classes."—*Nonconformist.*

" Here is an excellent temperance tale from the pen of a ready and powerful writer, issued by a publisher not connected with the temperance movement. The tale is one of great interest, and deserves the hearty patronage of the temperance public."—*The Temperance Record.*

" The thief here pourtrayed is that very insidious one, drink—or the habit of drinking—which, in truth, robs a man of everything. Written for humble folks, by one of themselves, the story cannot fail to have a good and wholesome influence among the class for whom it is intended. One good feature in it, as distinguished from temperance stories generally, is that, though it paints the drunkard's fate as black as possible, it restores him repentant to his friends and to his position in society."—*Standard.*

" A very remarkable tale concerning a man who, being in a respectable situation, lost it, and brought himself and his family to ruin by drunkenness ; and afterwards recovered himself by total abstinence. . . . . . The author displays considerable power of narration, and carries the reader along with unflagging interest to the end. . . . . We should be glad to see a new and cheaper edition obtaining (what it well deserves) a large circulation. The graphic faculty of the author, as displayed in more than one character and scene, should be cultivated and encouraged, and particularly when it is exercised in a good cause." —*The Watchman.*

" This is described on the title page as 'A Tale for Humble Folks by One of Themselves,' but it may be read with interest by all conditions of people, and with advantage to some of them. The tale is told with genuine feeling always, and occasionally with a quaint humour which readers will admire. There are some admirably drawn characters introduced. . . . ."—*The News of the World.*

" This is a temperance tale of more than ordinary ability. . . . . He (the author) writes with an earnestness and vigour which cannot fail to make a profound impression on his readers. . . . . Many of the characters are well drawn, and much humour is developed in the sketch of Uncle Wood—a second edition, on a small scale, of the inimitable Captain Cuttle."—*The Leeds Mercury.*

" In plain and simple language, without the least attempt at literary art or adornment, the author of this brief story tells the history of a family of which he was the eldest son. The story is that of a clerk in humble circumstances, whose home consists of two rooms in the heart of the city of London. Here, with his young wife and two children, he enjoys much true domestic happiness, until he becomes acquainted with the 'insidious thief.' . . . . He falls; and the chapters in which this part of the story is told lead us to expect something much more carefully worked out, fuller in detail, and abounding in dramatic writing, from the pen of this author at a future day. . . . . The book is right in tone, and sufficiently entertaining to make readers desire a further acquaintance with its writer. Temperance people ought to have their attention called to the *Insidious Thief*, which will form an excellent addition to the stock of tales advocating their principles."— *The Derby Mercury.*

"The style is homely but graphic; the characters are clearly drawn: one of them, Uncle Wood, is decidedly an original. . . . The interest of the tale is well sustained, and the lesson taught will, no doubt, make it as useful as it is entertaining."—*The Alliance News.*

"'The Insidious Thief' is a well-told temperance story—not much as a tale, and failing of poetical justice; but excellently and skilfully pointing a moral. It is evidently written by one well acquainted with life, and possessing considerable literary skill. We should rejoice for it to find its way to the home of every working man, and of many who, like the hero, move in a higher sphere of social life."—*British Quarterly Review.*

"That a second edition of a book, written by an unknown pen, has been called for in the course of a very few months—nay, of not many weeks, is a circumstance to provoke curiosity, if not to induce respect.

"The great feature and fault of all temperance tales written down to the 'League' level is, the necessity which seems laid upon the authors to make *all* their *dramatis personæ* live, and move, and have their being in an atmosphere of drink. The effect, if not morally appalling, is at least physically nauseating. . . . The 'Insidious Thief' is a story written in avowed hostility to strong drink; but it conducts the campaign after other tactics than those of the 'Hope Brigade.' . . . One thing about the present story stands forth in happy contrast to the general destruction assigned to victims in temperance tales: the unhappy prey seems to be rescued from the clutch at last, and the book sets with the gentle mellow light of peace upon the page.

"Natural, graphic, with an imploring pathos, and a *naive*, human-hearted inspiration, the story is on the whole excellent. It can hardly fail to do good; it cannot by any possibility do ill. . . . The great, the engrossing character, is the presiding good genius of the scene, Uncle Wood, an old 'salt.' He has a strong resemblance to the redoubted 'Captain Cuttle,' is every whit as *outré*, and has, every throb, as kind a heart. . . . . .

"An acquaintance with this novel no one can regret, whatever his principles, whatever his position."—*The Stirling Journal and Advertiser.*

Samuel Tinsley 10, Southampton Street, Strand.

PUTTYPUT'S PROTÉGÉE;

OR,

ROAD, RAIL, AND RIVER:

A HUMOROUS STORY IN THREE BOOKS.

BY HENRY GEORGE CHURCHILL.

1 Vol. Crown 8vo (uniform with "The Mistress of Langdale Hall"), wit
14 Illustrations by WALLIS MACKAY. Post free, 4s. Second Edition.

THE FOURTEEN FULL-PAGE ILLUSTRATIONS.

1. The Voyage of Discovery (Frontispiece).
2. The Escape from Bortonbrook Ayslum (Vignette).
3. In a Garret near the Sky.
4. The Happy Family.
5. The Road ! Hunted Down ! Gone Away.
6. The Lucky Number.
7. Bob Bembrow's Party.
8. Bob and Dollops.
9. The Devonsherry-Brothers.
10. A Waif from the Ocean.
11. Slitherem thinks Half a Loaf better than no Bread.
12. The Dissolution of Partnership.
13. The Particular Purpose.
14. The River ! All's Well that Ends Well.

"Admirably got up as regards paper, printing, and binding. . . .
Readable and interesting; very much superior to the ordinary ruck of
rubbish which loads the shelves of the circulating libraries."—*Court
Circular.*

"There is a class of readers that this novel will suit to a nicety.   It
is full of incidents and episodes.   For those fond of light reading it
possesses peculiar advantages.   If it be true, as we often hear, that
tastes differ on most subjects, there will be considerable difference of
opinion as to the merits of 'Puttyput's Protégée.' "—*Weekly Times.*

"It is impossible to read 'Puttyput's Protégée' without being reminded
at every turn of the contemporary stage, and the impression it leaves on
the mind is very similar to that produced by witnessing a whole
evening's entertainment at one of our popular theatres."—*Echo.*

Samuel Tinsley, 10, Southampton Street, Strand.

NOTICE.

Just published, in one handsome volume, with Frontispiece and
Vignette by PERCIVAL SKELTON.   Price Four Shillings, post free.

THE

MISTRESS OF LANGDALE HALL:

A ROMANCE OF THE WEST RIDING.

BY ROSA MACKENZIE KETTLE,

Author of "Smugglers and Foresters," "Fabian's Tower," etc.

(From THE SATURDAY REVIEW.)

Generally speaking, in criticising a novel we confine our observations
to the merits of the author.   In this case we must make an exception,
and say something as to the publisher.   The *Mistress of Langdale Hall*
does not come before us in the stereotyped three-volume shape, with
rambling type, ample margins, and nominally a guinea and a half to
pay.   On the contrary, this new aspirant to public admiration appears
in the modest guise of a single graceful volume, and we confess that
we are disposed to give a kindly welcome to the author, because we
may flatter ourselves that she is in some measure a *protégée* of our own.
A few weeks ago an article appeared in our columns censuring the
prevailing fashion of publishing novels at nominal and fancy prices.
Necessarily, we dealt a good deal in commonplaces, the absurdity of the
fashion being so obvious.   We explained, what is well known to every
one interested in the matter, that the regulation price is purely illusory.
The publisher in reality has to drive his own bargain with the libraries,
who naturally beat him down.   The author suffers, the trade suffers,
and the libraries do not gain.   Arguing that a palpable absurdity must
be exploded some day unless all the world is qualified for Bedlam, we

felt ourselves on tolerably safe ground when we ventured to predict an approaching revolution. Judging from the preface to this book, we may conjecture that it was partly on our hint that Mr. Tinsley has published. As all prophets must welcome events that tend to the speedy accomplishment of their predictions, we confess ourselves gratified by the promptitude with which Mr. Tinsley has acted, and we heartily wish his venture success. He recognises that a reformation so radical must be a work of time, and at first may possibly seem to defeat its object. For it is plain that the public must first be converted to a proper regard for its own interests ; and, by changing the borrowing for the buying system, must come in to bear the publisher out. He must look, moreover, to the support and imitation of his brethren of the trade. We doubt not he has made the venture after all due deliberation, and that we may rely on his determination seconding his enterprise. All prospectuses of new undertakings tend naturally to exaggeration, but success will be well worth the waiting for, should it be only the shadow of that on which Mr. Tinsley reckons. He gives some surprising figures ; he states some startling facts ; and, as a practical man, he draws some practical conclusions. He quotes a statement of Mr. Charles Reade's, to the effect that three publishers in the United States had disposed of no less than 370,000 copies of Mr. Reade's latest novel. He estimates that the profits on that sale—the book being published at a dollar—must amount to £25,000. Mr. Reade, of course, has a name, and we can conceive that his faults and blemishes may positively recommend themselves to American taste. But Mr. Tinsley remarks that if a publisher could sell 70,000 copies in any case, there would still be £5,000 of clear gain ; and, even if the new system had a much more moderate success than that, all parties would still profit amazingly. For Mr. Tinsley calculates the profits of a sale of 2,000 copies of a three-volume edition at £1,000, and we should fancy the experience of most authors would lead them to believe he overstates it. It will be seen that at all events the new speculation promises brilliantly, and reason and common sense conspire to tell us that the reward must come to him who has patience to wait. *Palmam qui meruit ferat,* and may he have his share of the profits too. Meanwhile, here we have the first volume of Mr. Tinsley's new series in most legible type, in portable form, and with a sufficiently attractive exterior. The price is four shillings, and, the customary trade deduction being made to circulating libraries, it leaves them without excuse should they deny it to the order of their customers.

Samuel Tinsley, 10, Southampton Street, Strand.

We should apologise to Miss Kettle for keeping her waiting while we discuss business matters with her publisher. But she knows, no doubt, that there are times when business must take precedence of pleasure and conscientious readers are bound to dispose of the preface before proceeding to the book. For we may say at once that we have found pleasure in reading her story. In the first place, it has a strong and natural local colouring, and we always like anything that gives a book individuality. In the next, there is a feminine grace about her pictures of nature and delineations of female character, and that always makes a story attractive. Finally, there is a certain interest that carries us along, although the story is loosely put together, and the demands on our credulity are somewhat incessant and importunate. The scene is laid in the West Riding of Yorkshire ; nor did it need the dedication of the book to tell us that the author was an old resident in the county. With considerable artistic subtlety she lays her scenes in the very confines of busy life. Cockneys and professional foreign tourists are much in the way of believing that the manufacturing districts are severed from the genuinely rural ones by a hard-and-fast line ; that the demons of cotton, coal, and wool blight everything within the scope of their baleful influence. There can be no greater blunder ; native intelligence might tell us that mills naturally follow water power, and that a broad stream and a good fall generally imply wooded banks and sequestered ravines, swirling pools, and rushing rapids. Miss Kettle, as a dweller in the populous and flourishing West Riding, has learned all that of course. She is aware besides of the power of contrast ; that peace and solitude are never so much appreciated as when you have just quitted the bustle of life, and hear its hum mellowed by the distance. Romance is never so romantic as when it rubs shoulders with the practical, and sensation "piles itself up" when it is evolved in the centre of commonplace life. . . . . . .

Although, however, the story unquestionably often loses in interest by the very efforts made to excite it, still it is interesting, and very pleasantly written, and for the sake of both author and publisher we cordially wish it the reception it deserves.

"The most careful mother need not hesitate to place it at once in the hands of the most unsophisticated daughter. As regards the publisher, we can honestly say that the type is clear and the book well got up in every way."—*Athenæum.*

"There is a naturalness in this novel, published in accordance with

Mr. Tinsley's very wholesome one-volumed system, which will attract many quiet readers. We will just express our satisfaction at the portable and readable size of the book."—*Spectator.*

"The Mistress of Langdale Hall" is a bright and attractive story, which can be read from beginning to end with pleasure."—*Daily News.*

"A charming 'Romance of the West Riding,' full of grace and pleasing incident. Miss Kettle's language is smooth without being forcible, and is quiet and sparkling, in character with the nature of her novel."—*Public Opinion.*

"The story itself is really well told, and some of the characters are delineated with great vividness and force. The tone of the book is high. The writer shows considerable mastery of her art."—*Nonconformist.*

"It is a good story, with abundant interest, and a purity of thought and language which is much rarer in novels than it ought to be. The volume is handsomely got up, and contains a well-drawn vignette and frontispiece."—*Scotsman.*

"Not only is it written with good taste and good feeling, it is never dull, while at the same time it is quite devoid of sensationalism or extravagance. It deals with life in the West Riding, and the descriptions of the authoress show a real affection for the rich woodlands and wild hills, and still more for the quaint old mansions of Yorkshire."—*Globe.*

"The book is admirably got up, and contains an introductory circular by the publisher."—*Civil Service Gazette.*

"The book is a model of what a cheap novel should be."—*Publishers' Circular.*

"A circular from the publisher precedes the opening of the novel, wherein the existing conditions of novel-publishing are concisely set forth. It is ably and smartly written, and forms by no means the least interesting portion of the contents of the volume. We strongly recommend its perusal to novel readers generally."—*Welshman.*

"Few will take up this entertaining volume without feeling compelled to go through with it. We cannot entertain a doubt as to the success of this novel, and the remarks made by the publisher in his prefatory circular are of the most sensible and practical kind."—*Hull Packet.*

"For this district the 'Mistress of Langdale Hall' has a peculiar interest."—*Leeds Mercury.*

Samuel Tinsley, 10, Southampton Street, Strand.

NOTICE—SECOND EDITION OF "ANOTHER WORLD."

In 1 vol. Post 8vo, price 12s.

ANOTHER WORLD;

or,

FRAGMENTS FROM THE STAR CITY OF MONTALLUYAH.

BY HERMES.

"A very curious book, very clearly written. . . . . Likely to contain hints on a vast number of subjects of interest to mankind."— *Saturday Review.*

"Hermes is a really practical philosopher, and utters many truths that must be as useful to this sublunary sphere as to those of another world. . . . Of his powers of narrative and expression there can be no doubt."—*Morning Post.*

"A romance of science. . . . Few volumes that have ever come under our hands are more entertaining to read or more difficult to criticise."—*Sunday Times.*

"We can recommend 'Another World' as decidedly clever and original."—*Literary World.*

"Whether one reads for information or for amusement, 'Another World' will attract and retain the attention. It reminds one somewhat of Swift's 'Gulliver,' without the grossness and the ill-nature."— *Standard.*

"'Another World' can be safely recommended as sure to afford amusement, combined with no little instruction."—*Echo.*

"'Hermes' is to be congratulated upon having written with much ingenuity and descriptive power. The book will doubtless attract, as, indeed, it deserves, a good deal of attention."—*Court Circular.*

". . . . We might quote much more, and fill many columns from this curious work, but we have, probably, said enough to stimulate the curiosity of our readers, who will, we have no doubt, speedily procure it, and pursue for themselves the fanciful and elaborate descriptions of the author. Many amusing and clever suggestions are embodied in its pages, and we cannot help suspecting that some of the ingenious speculations regarding the Star Worlds are intended by the author as good-humoured satires upon the familiar institutions of this hum-drum every-day life of ours."—*Era.*

Samuel Tinsley, 10, Southampton Street, Strand.

www.ingramcontent.com/pod-product-compliance
Lightning Source LLC
Chambersburg PA
CBHW020857020726
47497CB00005B/1448